THE SCALPER

THE SCALPER

RICHARD PROSCH

WHEELER PUBLISHING
A part of Gale, a Cengage Company

LIBRARY OF CONGRESS CIP DATA ON FILE.
CATALOGUING IN PUBLICATION FOR THIS BOOK
IS AVAILABLE FROM THE LIBRARY OF CONGRESS.

ISBN-13: 978-1-4328-9945-5 (softcover alk. paper)

Published in 2022 by arrangement with Richard Prosch

Printed in the United States of America
2 3 4 5 6   26 25 24 23 22

TABLE OF CONTENTS

The Scalper 9
Hester's Vanity 24
Eustace and Cats 37
Abram's Wife 51
Collecting Seamus O'Shaughnessy . . 59
Storm Damage 83
The Better Salesman 90
One Last Job 106
Tell Tail 109
Ida Tully and the Telephone. 122
Killing Hilda Kempker 139
AKA: The DaVinci Kid 155
Grand Design 174
The Mahogany Lily 187
Bird's-Eye View 191

ACKNOWLEDGEMENTS 197
ABOUT THE AUTHOR 199

For Grandpa Prosch,
who well knew western paperbacks

THE SCALPER

Fat Charlie McSnatt could feel the fish slipping off the hook. The old boy had nipped at the bait, but the hook wasn't solid, and now things were going south.

Charlie tasted breakfast bacon in his teeth, poked at it with his tongue while keeping his head down. He didn't blink. The fish was a man named Merkel, ramrod at the late Frank Jessup's place, and the bait was a pair of white-faced bucket calves.

"The heifer's a feisty one," said Charlie, giving the calf a nudge with his knee to prove the point. Feisty usually flavored the bait. The little heifer didn't move. Charlie pretended not to notice while he toed the barn floor's straw bedding. "She's a reg'lar whiz-bang."

The Jessup barn was a big, two-story affair, smelling of cows, fresh pine, and alfalfa hay. In the bright September morning, the red exterior had been a beacon calling to

Charlie as he followed the crick out of town with his rattle-trap wagon and his calves. He sold a dog to Merkel a couple years back. Charlie hoped to reel him again, but he hadn't reckoned on Merkel being such a hardcase.

Sunlight streamed in through the open rolling door, through the holes in Charlie's straw hat, and he lifted his eyes.

"Like I says, I got three more calves outside in the wagon, just like these two. By golly, I hate to let 'em go."

"You keep 'em then," said Merkel, flipping the mangled, wet butt of his spent cigar to the floor. He hooked his thumbs into his wide leather belt. "That un's got the scours," he said. "Hope it don't spread to our own." Merkel held up his calloused hands. "Damn it, Charlie, you're a good man, but it seems that as soon as a man buys something from you, he buries it."

The hell. Charlie waded in one more time. "I'll let you have all five of my calves for that yearling steer I seen when I came in."

"That what you call an even trade?" said Merkel.

The heifer calf took a sideways step, bumping its companion with a sickly bawl.

"Scours dry up," said Charlie, sounding almost as weak.

"Sanders told me you brought pink-eye down on his place last month." Merkel chuckled. "And him a veterinarian. It took some stones to pull that one off."

"Wasn't me, sir," said Charlie. "No sir. No pink eye here." Charlie thought about one of the calves in his wagon outside, pictured its running eye and the flies already pestering.

Nothing left for him here.

Charlie turned his face outside, to the square-built corrals, the long ranch house with its clean, white siding. Up here along the Missouri, the Nebraska spring air was full of tree pollen and twirling maple whirli-gigs. Sixty years old and Charlie knew he'd never have a claim like the Jessup ranch, or a strong man like Merkel to manage it. Too many things had gone against him. His wife and son were long gone, flown across the west, out of his life.

The only thing Charlie had left alive was his trade.

He cleared his throat for good-byes when Merkel surprised him.

"Tell you what. I've always had a soft spot for you, Charlie. Didn't I buy that no-account coon hound off of you? Whyn't you go talk to the widow?" he said. "Now that Mr. Jessup's gone, she's looking to make some changes."

Charlie chewed the inside of his cheek, gave the house a quick glance, and tried to remember Mrs. Jessup in a sea of soft, elderly faces. Widow ladies were something of a specialty. If Merkel gave him direct access to the old gal, Charlie reckoned himself a cattle baron by suppertime.

"Well sure, sure," said Charlie, standing up tall, letting the smile loose. "What kinda deal you got in mind?"

Merkel walked Charlie out of the barn with an arm on his shoulder.

"The widow is looking to sell some property. You being the kind of salesman you are, I think Mrs. Jessup might take you on as an agent. She'd pay you a commission if you can find us a buyer. Would you be interested in that kind of job?"

"Oh, I'm your man, sir. By golly, yes indeed, I'm your man." Barely able to contain himself, Charlie wiped his mouth with the back of his hand. "Let me get these two calves back in the wagon."

Merkel didn't offer to help him.

After Charlie took care of the calves and made sure his horses had some water, he fell in step with Merkel, and they climbed the steep trail to the house. Mrs. Jessup herself stood at the washroom door to meet them. She was at least ten years older than Charlie, and probably ten times stronger, he thought. She wore sturdy jeans with braces and a canvas shirt, had her hair pulled back in a severe braid, not at all the demur septuagenarian he'd constructed from memory and imagination.

"My husband and I took this claim in 1870, right after statehood came to the territory," said Mrs. Jessup, once the three of them were settled in the parlor. "This was truly rough country back then, a god-forsaken place."

"I can just imagine," said Charlie, lifting the fragile china cup to his lips, careful not to dribble coffee down his chin.

Mrs. Jessup sat on a straw-filled daybed, its blue velvet upholstery held in place by dozens of flower-headed brads. The room around them was clean and orderly, almost austere in terms of decoration. There was only one coal oil lamp that could be called ornate. Otherwise the room seemed more bland than the interior of the barn.

"Here's how it was back then," continued the old lady. "We didn't have many neighbors, but them's we did have were like family. We were there for each other in times of trial and times of celebration. We proved up on our place the earliest, so it became sort of the centerpiece for the community. Our home was open to all, no obligations, no restrictions. Frank was our first county commissioner. Did you know that? Did you know Frank?"

"It was Charlie what sold us Leroy, that coon dog Frank loved," said Merkel.

"I hated that dog," said Mrs. Jessup.

"Still and all," said Merkel.

"Water under the bridge," said Mrs. Jessup, waving away the comment. "The point is that Frank and I had an obligation to the new settlers. We were obliged to provide a haven of safety and, yes, even culture. That's where you come in, Charlie."

"Me? Culture?" said Charlie.

"Maybe you better show him," said Merkel.

Mrs. Jessup stood and Charlie eagerly followed suit. But instead of walking outside, she turned toward the door that led into the living room.

To Charlie, it felt like a lead ball rolled through his stomach.

There weren't no cattle or real estate in the living room.

And what was this talk about culture?

"Here she is," said Mrs. Jessup.

She stood beside a square grand piano.

Seven feet long, four feet wide, the heavy

sun-bleached rosewood cabinet stood on elephant legs covered in floral ornamentation. The dusty lid was closed, like a massive dark coffin, hiding unseen moldering entrails. But the ebony and ivory keys still gleamed in the sun, and there was no mistaking the ornate gold leaf lettering across the front that read Steinway and Sons, New York.

"I . . . uh," Charlie stammered. "I ain't sure what to say. This is what you want me to sell? You want me to hock your piano?"

"With the railroad bypassing us, it's the lack of community that convinced me to sell. Nobody comes around anymore."

"What do you say, Charlie?"

It was a tall order.

Charlie's wagon wasn't nearly big enough to carry the monstrous box.

He would need to describe the piece to prospective buyers in meticulous detail.

Arrange appointments with Mrs. Jessup.

Drive customers to and from the Jessup ranch to show it off.

"But I don't know a blessed thing about music," he said.

"You don't know a lot about beef cattle either, but that never stopped you," said Merkel. "Trust me. You're the man for the job."

"What are you asking for it?"

"Whatever you can get," said Mrs. Jessup. "Between you and me, the thing has outlived its usefulness. It's big and inconvenient to work around. Mostly I'm satisfied just to have somebody come move it regardless of what they pay."

Charlie had to admit he liked the sound of that. Maybe a chance to skim a little extra for himself.

He studied the heavy wood finish, the arrangement of the keys.

Steinway and Sons, by golly!

Why not try? Wasn't this a chance to move up?

Charlie could be a real salesman, a respectable professional.

Not what everybody called him.

No more just an old scalper.

"There's only one thing," said Mrs. Jessup. "It doesn't play. Frank had the keys and action out to work on it, and that damned coon hound ate the hammers. We can slide the keys out and look at it if you want."

"It doesn't play?" said Charlie.

"Insides ain't nothing but a mess of splinters. And it's missing a few wires, too."

"I'm sure there's somebody who could —"

"There's a good-sized crack in the cabinet

16

back here," said Mrs. Jessup, lifting the lid a smidge to point out a pine board patch nailed to the inside of the case. "Did my best to hold her together with a few pegs."

"Selling half-dead critters is right up Charlie's alley," said Merkel. "Maybe talk to that music professor over at the new college."

The coffee sloshed around in Charlie's stomach, and he edged toward the door.

But still, the job offered a certain prestige, so he took it.

From now on, he'd be revered as Charles McSnatt, Seller of Steinway Pianos and Other Fine Instruments. Nobody needed to know more than that.

The first thing was to print up a series of flyers.

In lavish copy, Charlie praised the Jessup piano's gorgeous rosewood case (what there was of it) and the polished ebony and ivory keys. He tried to play up the notoriety of the Steinway name and its place in American history. He used the human-interest angle too, how Mrs. Jessup, a pillar among Nebraska pioneers, could only now part with the piece because of her husband's death, and how much it had meant to her and the community.

He didn't mention that it was broken beyond repair.

Three weeks later, he still didn't have a single offer.

Again, he stood with Merkel inside the door of the barn. This time the sky was full of heavy clouds.

"Them's that wants a piano already has one. Them's that don't, well you couldn't give it to them," said Charlie.

"Did the widow mention you could toss in all her sheet music? She's got a bunch of ol' sheet music."

"Almost had one young fellar," said Charlie, ignoring him. He held his thumb and forefinger close together. "Kid was that close to buying when he asked about the spools." Charlie pulled a face. "Spools? What spools, I asked him. Player spools, he says." Charlie shook his head. "Kid thought it was one of them automatic playing pianos. Wanted it for a new establishment up by the reservation."

Charlie shook his head and looked around the Jessup place.

This time it didn't seem so grand. Maybe it was the dribbly gray light. You could see the sloppy brush strokes on the red barn. The house looked more yellow than white, and one of the rain gutters was busted loose.

"Maybe we ought to just let this thing go," said Charlie.

"You of all people giving up," said Merkel. "This ain't the old Fat Charlie talking."

"What would you have me do?"

Merkel lit a fresh cigar.

"You talk to that professor over at the college? They got what they call a music conservatory over there. You ought to talk to him." Merkel blew a cloud of smoke high into the air.

"Too late," said Charlie. "The way I hear it, that old bird's not long for the world." Charlie shook his head. "No, no. It's hopeless."

"I think you're trying too hard to be a piano salesman," said Merkel. "You're trying to be something you're not."

Charlie looked at Merkel straight. "So what exactly am I?"

"You're the man that could sell pink-eye to a veterinarian. That's who you are. Exactly what that makes you, I ain't qualified to judge. But it's a rare talent."

Charlie raised his eyebrows. He'd never really thought about it that way.

Merkel slapped him on the shoulder. "Why not get on with it, man? Get creative, damn you."

■ ■ ■ ■

A week later, Charlie drove his wagon right up to Mrs. Jessup's door. After helping his dark-suited passenger down, he waved a friendly arm in Merkel's direction. Down beside the barn, his pitchfork full of hay, Merkel nodded.

"We've come about the piano," called Charlie.

"Be with you in a minute," said Merkel.

Charlie nodded and reached out to help his guest up the trail. The tall man took small steps, his black lace boots almost shuffling along, his long black coat catching sandburs on the fringe.

"I'm sure you'll be well pleased, doctor," said Charlie. "Well pleased."

Before long, the men stood beside the Steinway and faced Mrs. Jessup. The stranger held his top hat in hand, revealing a round pate with three combed-over black locks.

"This is Dr. Robards," said Charlie. "He's with the college."

Mrs. Jessup shook Robards' hand. "How nice to meet you." Robards nodded.

Merkel held out his hand. "I'm the one suggested Charlie talk to you."

"Indeed?" said Robards.

"This here's the piece I was telling you about," Charlie said, sweeping his arm wide to encompass the piano.

Robards put his hand to his chin, shuffled carefully around, his black eyes taking in every aspect of the instrument, from the keys to the case, the carved legs to the lid.

"It's exquisite. Just the thing we've been looking for," said Robards.

"And the, uh . . . the price we agreed on is still fine?"

Robards stood beside Charlie and nodded. "Yes, yes, fine indeed." From inside his coat he produced a slip of paper.

"One thousand dollars," he said, and handed the check to Mrs. Jessup. "I believe this is yours."

Mrs. Jessup's mouth momentarily dropped. Then she gave Robards a broad smile and turned to Charlie. He felt himself blush at the look of admiration.

"Pleasure to do business with you men," said Merkel, reaching for Charlie's hand. "A real pleasure."

"The timing makes it worth the money," said Robards. "A real Steinway. And precisely when we needed it."

"I'm so glad," said Mrs. Jessup.

"Charlie here was able to name his price."

After the arrangements had been made for moving the piano, Charlie led Robards back to the wagon.

"One minute," said Merkel from the door stoop.

Charlie didn't like the look on the ramrod's face. Excusing himself, he left Robards to wait.

"What? What?"

"You and me just need to be clear on the commission," said Merkel. "I already told the widow it's okay with me if you get something out of this. But at least half that agent's fee is mine."

"Yours?" Charlie wrinkled his brow. "I'm not following you."

"Ain't I the one said you needed to talk to that old music professor at the college?"

Charlie nodded. "You did say that. But this ain't him."

"Huh? What are you trying to pull? You introduced that man as somebody with the college."

"Oh, yes, Dr. Robards is with the college," said Charlie. "But the man you told me to contact about using the piano as a musical instrument, well . . . he died."

"Died?"

"God rest 'im," said Charlie. "I told you he wasn't long for the world."

"So who's this Robards person?"

"He's with the administration."

"It don't make no difference. Either way, the college gets the piano. You owe me."

"Well, actually, no. The college won't be using the piano."

Merkel scratched his head, and Charlie continued. "Our Dr. Watkins, the music professor, had no family. So he left it up to the board of directors to make final arrangements. One of his final wishes was that he be committed to the earth in a way that reflected his years of musicianship."

Merkel smiled then, as Charlie's words hit home.

"You mean?"

Charlie nodded. "Now, if you'll let me get back to my passenger.

No wonder Robards was happy about the timing of the sale. No wonder Charlie could name his price.

"Always did say that as soon as a man buys something from you, he buries it," said Merkel.

"I'll be back next week for my commission," said Charlie.

HESTER'S VANITY

In Atlas Sam's tent saloon outside Camp Stambaugh, Herman told his friends about the wife. "I swear it happened almost overnight, her puttin' up these picture frames all over the place — over the sink, over the fireplace, two or three on the bedroom wall."

Herman never saw so many picture frames in his life, and he hadn't mentioned most of them.

"She's got one strung up in the privy," he said.

Sam just nodded a bushy head over the problem. His silence urged Herman on.

"Got a couple factory-made pieces," Herman said, "but most of 'em she made by hand out of sticks and grass. Got more frames than pictures.

"She even put one frame around a patch in the sod wall. She says it looks like the profile of her dead sister, the way she remembers her sitting at church."

"What's it look like to you?" said Sam.

"I don't think her sister's whiskers were that long."

Sam chuckled, then let it go. Herman took a long drink from his tin cup.

"The other night she put a by-God picture frame around the tea kettle," he said. "Just set it up around the kettle, sayin' it shows off the candle light better."

"Just an empty frame?" said Sam.

Herman nodded. "Just an empty frame. Tell you the truth, I'm a little bit afraid to sit still, scared she's gonna put one around me one of these days."

Herman didn't tell Sam what else Hester said — that come summer she was going to start making her own drawings. On store-bought paper. She'd already been to Atlantic City and talked to Glen Burris at his telegraph, sent away for a big fat roll of "fine bleached pulp," not bothering to tell Herman what "fine bleached pulp" was going to cost. He knew anything with the word "fine" in it was going to cost a dang sight more than a sheep man could regular afford.

He tried not to chew on it.

Herman figured the long Wyoming winter had made Hester a little loopy, and he hoped the hot summer winds would blow

25

up a cure. In the meanwhile, he spent most of his time playing Pitch with Sam and Willy Three-Eyes.

By the first of June, Hester was sketching on the backs of flour sacks with charcoal and ash from the stove while she waited for her mail-order paper.

"I drove that darned freight back and forth from the train to South Pass City for seven years," Herman told his friends the night he got back from the station. "Started in the fall of '68 and every day dreaming of my own spread. Here I am ten years later, got some land to my name, animals of my own, and now that Hester's got me going back and forth to the rail so often, I'm feeling like an old teamster again."

The railroad station at Point of Rocks was a long ride to the south.

Sam looked over Herman's shoddy outfit. "How old is that horse?" he said.

Herman ignored him.

"What'cha got in there?" said Willy, gripping the side rail with stubby, split fingers and standing on tiptoe to peer over the edge of the wagon.

"None of your business," said Herman, but his friend had seen the wood frames and the roll of butter-colored paper.

"Guess you picked all that up for Hester," said Willy, combing out his gray beard.

"The world was a lot better place before the idea of mail order," said Herman. He was in a philosophical mood. "Glen Burris tells me everything can be delivered right to your door. Well, I told him what I think."

"What'd you tell him?" said Willy.

"I think folks don't hardly have to work for it. Just order it up and there it is in front of 'em."

Willy nodded grimly. "What good is it if you don't work for it?"

"Every day I dreamed of my own spread," said Herman.

"Lots of men 'round the Sweetwater dreamed," said Sam, muttering under his breath. Herman figured his friend didn't want to offend Willy. The old-timer had been at the gold mines since '69 and, other than dust and a stray nugget here or there, he'd yet to find a blessed thing.

"I never had the itch like that," said Herman. "Never worried about gold." He gave Willy a sympathetic look.

Herman's luck had gone the other way. He won his sod house ranch in a card game in '75, livestock included.

"I wanted to build something with my own hands," said Herman. "Have a wife."

He courted Hester for ten days. When her sister married Glen Burris, Herman suggested they take advantage of the church already being rented and tie the knot themselves.

Hester said she had nothing better to do. Six weeks later, her sister passed away. Hester never talked about it.

"I hoped Hester and me might have a family by now," said Herman.

Three years gone and Herman had a dozen more sheep, the picture frames, and twenty-odd charcoal drawings of his dead in-law.

"I just don't understand her," said Herman. "Last night she put a frame around some shadows on the floor and just kept givin' them the bug-eye. Like she wasn't happy with 'em being the way they was."

Inside the tent, each of the men had a drink and agreed the old girl was inscrutable.

In August, Herman found some money rolled up with a piece of twine in Hester's basket. When he asked her about it, Hester wouldn't say a word. When he told Willy Three-Eyes, the old prospector gave it to him straight.

"It was from my own Emma," he said.

"Payment for one of them drawings. Emma's got it hanging up right beside the door," said Willy. "Not sure what it's supposed to be, but Emma sure enough thinks it's pretty."

Atlas Sam shook his head and poured fresh libations. "I never heard of somebody selling a drawing before."

Herman waved him off. "They do it all the time," he said. "If you're any good at all you make a living at it." He took his drink in one swallow, put the glass down too hard. "In France, or wherever." Again he waved his hand back and forth, swatting away the details.

"Ain't important," said Willy.

Herman pulled a bag of fresh tobacco from his pocket and built a smoke.

"They're pulling out the last of the cavalrymen next week," said Sam.

What they'd known all summer was finally coming to pass. With the gold mining business a bust and the Indians tamed, Camp Stambaugh was shutting down.

"Who needs 'em?" said Willy.

"It's vanity is what it is," said Herman.

"What?" said Willy.

"Hester's drawing. It's all vanity."

"All is vanity," said Sam. "What profit hath a man of all his labor which he taketh under the sun?"

"Huh?" said Herman.

"It's from the Good Book," said Sam. "Ecclesiastes."

"I never took you for much of a Bible thumper," said Herman.

"He's practicing," said Willy. "Sam's got his eye on the Reverend Dawson's daughter."

"That's not so," said Sam, folding his big mitts together on the table. "I happen to enjoy reading the scriptures. Did you know Ecclesiastes means *teacher* in American?"

Herman spit in his hand and doused his quirly there.

He felt glum.

Everything in the basin was changing.

A few days later Hester sold another picture. This time it was a full-color painting for a soldier's wife. Herman decided it was pure sentiment on the customer's part, a souvenir from the lonely frontier outpost. Herman imagined that once she got back east, the woman would stash the thing away in an attic for her great-grandchildren to dispose of.

When winter came for good in early November, the friends moved their drinking from the tent to Sam's one-room shack. "Cold as it is, Hester sits outside and draws pictures of the mountains," said Herman after his last hand of cards. "Sometimes she leaves the ranch. Says she's following the sunlight. Last week she took the horse and wagon and left for the whole day."

"Maybe she'll run out of paper," said Willy.

"Nope. She put in a new order with Glen Burris last week," said Herman. "More of everything. Charcoal pencils. Cakes of hard paint. She's got her own money."

"She's seeing a lot of young Burris," said Sam.

"What of it? Him operating the telegraph and being her brother-in-law after all," said Herman.

"Ex-brother-in-law, you mean," said Sam. "Seeing as the sister's dead."

"God rest her," Willy added.

"I was talking about Hester's drawing," said Herman.

"Are they any good?" said Sam.

Herman noticed Sam downed two shots of rye for every one he swallowed.

"What do you mean?" said Herman.

"I mean do you think Hester's drawings are any good?" said Sam, his voice rising. "Have you taken the time to look at them? You'd think she must be pretty good after

31

all these months of practice."

"You're in a temper," said Herman. "And you don't even have a wife to send you around the bend."

Willy whispered the news. "He ain't getting one either. The preacher's daughter done eloped with a Laramie man."

"I just think you ought to quit complaining over her," said Sam. "You ain't never done nothing to deserve her."

Herman slid his chair back. "Look, now," he said.

"No, I mean it," said Sam. "All you do is complain about her while she does your cookin' and cleanin' and washin' up, and she still has time to create all this wonderful beauty —"

"Sam?" said Willy.

"And you who gambled and lied and got lucky —"

"Sam," said Herman.

"You ain't accomplished half what she has," said Sam.

Then Herman saw the small framed rectangle hanging just beside Sam's bed.

For just a minute, he recognized what it was: the Oregon Buttes, their thick shadows and lush ochers as seen through Hester's eye, their sweeping façade cast in eternal autumn by her practiced hand.

A second later, it looked more or less like a kitchen accident.

"I've got to be going," said Herman.

He hoped by slamming the door on his way out, the painting would fall.

But he didn't think it did.

A few days later, Herman borrowed Willy's horse and, at a good distance, followed Hester through the ramshackle storefronts of Atlantic City, then farther, back around to the edge of their own ranch, where the Willow Creek flowed under a thin crust of snow.

Herman still couldn't quite grip what was going on in the woman's head. He hoped by watching her, he would begin to understand how to live with it.

How to stop it.

When he came around a wall of granite to an empty, frosted grassland, he stomped his feet. He'd lost her. Turning toward home, he came across one of his own shepherds.

The Basque's name was Ibarra, and his dog sat beside the wagon tongue without barking. Herman didn't speak Ibarra's language, but a lot of the sheep men developed a crude sign language with the herders, and since the topic of conversation usually had only to do with the sheep, they got so they understood each other fairly well.

Herman poked his head into Ibarra's wagon, putting some real authority into his voice.

"You seen my wife?"

As it was, Ibarra had no idea what Herman was talking about.

Helplessly, he shook his head.

But Herman wasn't looking at the shepherd.

Pinned to the canvas wagon cover, three scraps of paper fluttered in the wind. Again, Herman saw his wife's hand on display. Here was Willow Creek in bold, vibrant strokes. There was the granite pyramid he'd just passed, its component stones rendered with looping spirals, its foundation held in place with heavy shadows.

Herman blinked, and the pictures stayed steady and as clear as the tintypes they used to display at the camp.

"Where is she?" he said again. But then he remembered what day it was in the week, so he turned and rode away before there was any chance of an answer.

Herman's thoughts were headed in a terrible direction.

He stopped at his soddy long enough to pick up some water, provisions for his horse. And a gun.

Then he rode for Point of Rocks.

He rode through the night, stopping only long enough to rest his horse.

But it didn't matter.

When he got there, the train was a smudge of brown and white on the horizon.

Herman stood beside Willy's horse at the edge of the station and watched it go. Shading his eyes, he let a finger drop and the train disappeared. He lifted his finger, and the train reappeared. Funny how something that appeared so small could, in reality, be so big.

Perspective was hard for Herman to figure.

He crossed the boardwalk and stepped into the office. Glen Burris wasn't there.

"Figured you might be along," said a heavy man at the desk. He stood up and shook hands with Herman. "I'm new here. Name is Tanner."

"How do you know me?" said Herman, his eyes darting around the room.

Owl Creek mountain sat on the desk in a braided grass frame.

"Mr. Burris described you. Told me to expect you," said Tanner.

An unnamed procession of hills dappled with umber and green hung on the wall in a frame of lashed aspen twigs.

"The lady asked me to give you this," said Tanner, handing over an envelope.

Herman stared hard at the string tie. He opened it with trembling fingers and pulled out Hester's masterpiece.

It was the inside of the soddy.

Hester had captured it all in precise detail. The woodstove, the fire, the picture frames. Sure enough, she had the tea kettle just right.

The open room they shared, and the life they hadn't.

For the first time, Herman openly admired his wife's work.

"Look at the detail there in that chair," he told Tanner, pointing at the paper. "Look at how real that tea kettle looks, framed just so."

That Hester was some kind of artist.

Well, that's what she was all right. "She's an artist," he said.

Herman held the drawing at arm's length and smiled even as tears came down his cheeks.

He couldn't help but notice that the room in the drawing was empty.

Like it would be when he got home.

Like it would always be.

EUSTACE AND CATS

Six miles away from the stagecoach line and Eustace Novacek, a man who liked living alone on the Nebraska frontier, still couldn't visit the privy in peace. He was used to the breeze whistling through the vertical cracks of the leaning frame outhouse, and he didn't mind the snow accumulating in the corners. But on a winter's night, when the wood smoke from his cabin got lost in the wind before it could cover the stink of the latrine below and the temperature dropped faster than his pants, he shouldn't have to share an evening constitutional with a needy, pestering varmint.

Again, the white paw came under the door from outside.

Followed by a plaintive wail.

Then the paw through the moonlit crack.

Poke.

Poke.

Eustace threw another corn cob at the

doorjamb.

Damn cat.

Eustace slumped down on the rough-cut hole in the privy bench, canvas trousers around his ankles, tattered coyote fur shirt covering his chest.

The paw came again, trying to get his attention. And the meow.

Running short on cobs, Eustace did his best to ignore it.

Eustace hated cats.

Naturally, after he'd finished his business, the cat was there, waiting for him with its breath coming in little frozen clouds, prancing around through the snow, threatening to trip Eustace up when he trudged toward the house.

"G'wan! Get out of here," he told the fat gray tiger-stripe.

He didn't waste his time kicking at the thing.

Anything less than a lead pellet was useless.

And God only knew where she came from.

The way she hung around, and the size of her, made him think she was somebody's stray pet.

"Half a dozen miles from nowhere, in the middle of the Sandhills. You're a damned long way from home," he told her.

At the door, the cat shot between his legs, hoping to slip into the cabin. But Eustace could move quick, too, and he slammed the door in her face.

The cat offered a complaining wail, but Eustace ignored her.

He walked to his kitchen table, a thick slab of roughhewn oak and, sitting down, shuffled a deck of cards.

He'd been good at cards once. Good with a gun.

Eustace eyed the big Colt in its dry leather holster hanging from a peg beside the door.

Lately he'd been thinking about picking the gun up again.

Maybe hit the Tuesday stage this month when it carried the payroll box.

Then maybe retire to Texas like he always wanted. Like him and the Granger boys used to talk about.

Outside, the cat howled, but Eustace didn't hear it.

He was too busy thinking about the heist, dreaming about his comeback.

After she caught a mouse in the haybarn and carried it to his steps, Eustace named the cat Yardbird and started to regularly share his supper scraps with her.

If you can't beat 'em, feed 'cm.

But not too many scraps.

Just enough to keep her around. Not so many she'd fall down on the job mousing.

Eustace hated mice worse than cats.

One day, after a week of feeding Yardbird, he noticed she wasn't so fat anymore. In fact, she was rail thin.

She must've had a litter of kittens.

How many?

Standing in his open doorway, sipping a tin of coffee and warming his face with morning sun, Eustace watched the cat trek across the muddy path to the barn. Every couple feet she'd stop and lift her paws, shaking off the mud with obvious irritation. One time she looked back at him in the cabin door as if he were to blame for her discomfort.

He shrugged, saluting her with his cup.

"Haybarn makes a good nursery," he said to himself. Then he went back to the table where he planned his raid on the stagecoach.

It ought to be a simple thing. He and the Grangers used to be pretty good at this kind of job. And nobody expected a hold-up way out here.

He planned to rob the stage at ten o'clock the next morning.

He spent a long time cleaning his gun and

oiling up the holster.

As time wore on, the temperature dropped, which actually suited Eustace. Snow was the only thing stopped the stage, and when it got real cold it generally didn't snow.

Eustace daydreamed about how he'd wait at the Willow Creek curve. How he'd jump out in front of the coach, gun blazing fire. How his face would be masked, and his black Stetson pulled low.

Within 24 hours, he'd be a rich man, ready to ride for Texas.

Which made him think he ought to check his horse.

Once outside, he found out the haybarn wasn't such a good nursery after all.

Just opposite the gelding's pen, Eustace found Yardbird nesting in a pumpkin-sized hollow of musty hay. Without so much as a twitch at his sudden appearance, she looked up at him through amber-green eyes full of weary resignation.

Three balls of fur lay near her belly: one a tiger-striped short hair, one a darker gray, and finally, a still, yellow runt seemingly cast off to the side. While Eustace watched them, the darker kittens wiggled and tugged at Yardbird's belly, but the yellow one didn't move.

Scrawny Yardbird might nurse two kittens. No way she had milk enough for three.

Before he could stop himself, Eustace scooped up the yellow kitten. It wasn't dead . . . yet, so he carried it into the house. While he boiled water in a pan, he put the furball in an old pewter dish that used to belong to his ma.

He named the cat Buttercup.

He didn't know spit about resurrecting a frozen cat, but something made him want to try.

It was a long night.

Buttercup was hardly bigger than a circus peanut and Eustace was careful to be gentle. He ran warm water through the kitten's icy fur and gently stroked her fragile legs of bone.

At first, she wouldn't take any of the canned milk he tried to feed her. But with patience and an eyedropper Eustace found in his old warbag, she slowly came around.

By morning, Buttercup made a pathetic mewling, barely audible, but a good sign.

The sun rolled into the frigid sky. Eustace yawned and checked his pocket watch.

Pert'near time to buckle on his gun, tie his mask to his neck, and get the gelding saddled up for the Willow Creek curve. Pert'near time for the robbery that would set him up for life.

But Buttercup wasn't out of the woods.

Eustace chose to boil some more water.

And by the time he'd given Buttercup a warm bath and another few drops of milk, it was ten, and he missed the stage.

"There'll be other opportunities," he told himself.

But that night in bed, listening to the little runt mewl away, he wanted to toss Buttercup back outside.

Who knows how much was in that payroll box? How much had he lost on account of a stupid cat?

What a dummy he was.

"I'll get another chance," he said again.

And it turns out he was right.

Several weeks later, Jonah Butcher stopped by to jawbone and do some trading. Eustace let Jonah have a few tins of tomatoes and some cornmeal in exchange for a big stack of newspapers, a chicken, and a box of canned milk.

With Buttercup established as a permanent resident of the cabin, all three items were welcome.

That night, Eustace sat up reading while the kitten curled up in its fruit crate box beside the stove.

A new bank had opened up nearby, and

their hours were posted on page three.

The ad boasted the brand name of the bank's vault.

Eustace smiled.

It was the kind of vault he'd broken into before.

Planning for a Sunday morning break-in, he carried his chicken bones out to the hay-barn for the other cats.

By now, with warmer weather in the off-ing, Yardbird was more active and her two dark kittens had left the barn, following her to the cabin once or twice.

They were still wild and ran away if Eustace looked at them cross-eyed. So he looked at them cross-eyed quite a bit.

But it was good having them out there.

The mouse population was down, the gelding was more calm than ever before, and Eustace didn't feel so lonely.

Every night, while Eustace dreamed of liv-ing the good life in Texas, Buttercup slept on the bed.

When Sunday morning came, Eustace was up before dawn.

While Buttercup roamed around the cabin playing with an old sock he'd given her for a toy, making various cat sounds, Eustace checked his gun and strapped on his belt.

After making sure the kitten had food and

44

water, he locked the cabin door behind him and went to the haybarn to saddle up.

He and the horse weren't 100 feet down the trail when Eustace saw Yardbird and her two offspring trailing along behind.

"Get home," he yelled. "Go on!"

Ignoring him, they continued along the trail, sniffing at the spring grass, pouncing on a fly.

Eustace figured they'd turn back once he outran 'em.

Spurring his horse down the road, he left the cats in a cloud of dust.

He shouldn't have stopped at the mile corner. He shouldn't have looked back.

Three dark specks were visible on the dusky morning road. In the clean, clear air, he could hear their meow.

What if they didn't turn back?

Eustace figured there was little chance Yardbird would get lost. But what about her kittens? The black one had a touch of ringworm and seemed a little shaky the last couple days.

He looked up at the brightening sky.

What if a hungry hawk came along?

He was planning to be back to the cabin before noon. He touched the gun in his holster. What if something happened to him?

Eustace wasn't used to thinking about

anybody else.

What would happen to Buttercup if he didn't get back?

Dammit.

Reluctantly, but knowing it was for the best, he turned back to the cabin.

When he rode past Yardbird, she didn't act like she noticed him.

Little snob.

But she was right there when he got back to the haybarn.

Late that night, Eustace woke from a deep sleep.

The gelding was restless, and Buttercup wasn't on the bed.

Plenty of moonlight poured through the window. Chancing a peek outside from the safety of his bed, Eustace couldn't see anything but the wide open hills with its familiar shadows.

The horse neighed again. Yardbird ran from the barn to the privy and back again.

Something had spooked them.

With Buttercup tearing up circles around the cookstove, Eustace pulled on his trousers and took his Colt down from its peg.

Quiet as he could, Eustace crept outside, the Colt surprisingly shaky in his sweaty grip.

"Hold on," he told himself. "Hold on there."

What was wrong with him? Trembling like a kitten for no good reason.

At this rate it was a good thing he hadn't tried robbing the bank.

Then he saw Yardbird back at the privy, crouched low, shoving her paw under the door, milking her claws on the old cedar wood.

Eustace froze.

Somebody was inside.

As he worked to calm his breathing and stay still, a groan came from the other side of the outhouse door.

It was a low sound, a gurgling noise. Not necessarily a man.

But what else?

Yardbird meowed and stitched a bounding path up and down around the little shack.

"C'mon out of there," said Eustace. "Whoever you are, you're trespassing."

No answer.

Yardbird ran to him, circled around his legs.

"Don't you worry," he told her. "I'm here."

Careful to keep his gun aimed straight at the outhouse door, Eustace bent down and picked up the cat in his left arm. She purred and rubbed her ears against the buckle of his suspender.

Whoever their visitor was, he was being awful quiet.

Or awful cagey.

"Get on out here, or I'll come in after you," said Eustace.

The normal night noise of the hills abruptly stopped. No crickets. No spring peepers.

Silence.

Maybe he'd try again.

Eustace let Yardbird jump to the ground, started to speak, and came face to face with an old friend as Dan Granger shoved his way through the privy door, a thundering six-gun in hand.

Eustace fell to the left, landing on his shoulder in a new-grown patch of thistle, while Dan stumbled forward, pulling the trigger again and again, slamming shot after shot into the gray moonlit sod before landing on his face.

Eustace was up in a hurry, finger on the trigger, but it was already over.

Dan Granger was spent as his weapon, a lifeless husk collecting the settling dust.

Yardbird meowed with curiosity.

"I don't know," said Eustace. "This here

fella used to be my friend."

Yardbird answered like she understood.

She stayed with him as he turned the body over to face the sky with unseeing eyes.

Dan's shirt was soaked through with blood.

"Been shot," said Eustace.

But not by him.

"Meow," said Yardbird.

Eustace followed her into the privy where he found a sack full of money. Some paper. Some coin.

"That vault," said Eustace. "The kind I used to know how to open. The kind Dan knew how to open, too."

Yardbird answered him.

Eustace nodded.

"You're right, girl," he said. "Poor old Dan read the same paper I did."

He watched the cat twitch her tail and stroll back toward the barn, the night's excitement already forgotten.

Slowly but surely, the two dark kittens poked their heads out of the barn.

Eustace looked back down at Dan.

Poor devil must've been out of his mind with pain. On the run, probably didn't even know where he was.

The Granger boys had the same Texas dream Eustace had.

And this is where it got Dan.

Before long, Eustace heard the sound of approaching horses.

He opened the cabin door, let Buttercup run into his arms, then sat down on the ground beside the body.

He scratched the kitten's ears, and she purred in response.

Then she rolled over in his lap and let him pet her belly.

When the posse arrived, they'd find Eustace here with his cats, the Texas dream waiting in the outhouse.

Where it probably always belonged.

Abram's Wife

Riding his buckskin gelding, deputy sheriff Whit Branham was delivering a package to Eden Valley when he saw Carlton Boggs and his wife, Greta, camped on the lush, green bank of Lassiter Crick.

He recognized them from the wanted poster hanging in his O'Neill, Nebraska, law office.

"That's them all right," said Branham's friend, Ezrie Dawson. "What'cha think we should do?"

Carlton Boggs leaned against a cedar pole wearing only a long nightshirt, his bare legs hardly keeping him upright. Sitting in the grass beside the wagon, Greta was shapely and blonde, wearing a man's shirt and trousers.

Their camp was a tidy affair on a patch of grass between the worn trail and the muddy track of the crick. Boggs had a pair of mules and a small, tattered covered wagon. Two or three feet in front of the lead wheel was the remnant of a fire with an old kettle sitting in the ashes.

Above them, a canopy of sycamore leaves played with light and shadow.

Neither of them appeared to be armed.

Branham's mustache, like his shoulder-length hair, was the color of rusty iron, and his Stetson matched the blue-black of the short-barrel coach shotgun in his saddle boot. "I'd hate to not get our package delivered," he said.

"Heavy as it is, I hate for your horse to keep lugging the dang thing around."

Branham glanced at the saddle bag behind his left hip where the big ornate book pushed aside an open flap.

"German heirloom," said Branham. "This book is real special to Clara's family."

"Good to do a favor for a friend," said Ezrie. "Biggest Bible I ever saw."

"Collected works of Shakespeare," said Branham. "Ain't no Bible."

Ezrie's reply was cut off by a call from the camp.

"Hello, Deputy!"

Boggs waved a knobby hand at the end of an upraised crooked right arm. "Join us for a spot of coffee?"

"Neighborly," said Branham, waving in return.

"Just you be ready for anything, Whit."

Branham grinned and spurred the buckskin forward.

Wasn't he always?

As it turned out he wasn't.

"You want me to do what?"

"Join me in the back of the wagon, Deputy," said Greta, green eyes sparkling in the sun as she moved across the shadow-dappled grass.

"Ma'am?" Branham said.

He felt the blood rushing to his cheeks even as he heard Boggs rasp, "It's all the same to me. You go ahead."

Greta crossed her arms.

Then pulled off her shirt.

Branham sat back in his saddle with an audible creak.

At the same time, Carlton Boggs found a surprise surge of energy and stepped away from his cedar crutch.

By the time Branham got his eyes away from naked Greta, Boggs had a big Colt revolver pulled from under his shirt and aimed at Branham's chest.

"Throw your gun over here, and then crawl down off the horse. Slow and steady, or I'll kill you both for sure."

Branham shoved his hat back on his head and slapped his thighs.

Well.

Damn.

Finally, he pulled the coach gun from its boot and tossed it to the ground.

"Lady, that's a dirty damn trick," he said.

"No trick," said Greta with a mischievous grin. She walked to the back of the wagon and started to climb inside. "You're welcome to join me." She smiled at Ezrie. "Both of you."

"I told you, it makes me no difference," said Boggs.

Branham laughed. "Oh, I think it does at that. I think it makes a big difference. Because if we're both in there with her, that leaves you free to pilfer my saddle bag."

With his bluff called, Boggs spoke to Greta. "C'mon and cover yourself up," he said. "Before you get skeeter bit."

Branham watched while the girl stepped down and got her shirt back on.

"You two remind me of that old story in the Good Book," he said. "What is it, Ezrie? The story of Lot's wife?"

"Lot's wife? I don't follow you."

"Shut up," said Boggs.

Branham ignored him.

"Yeah, Lot's wife. You know the story about the old fellar goes into strange country and pawns his wife off to the men so's to save his own skin."

"That ain't Lot," said Ezrie. "That's Abraham. But I think he was called Abram then."

"No," said Branham, shaking his head. "No, I'm sure it's Lot."

"I said, you shut up," said Boggs.

"What're they talking about?" said Greta. "How am I like this Lottie?"

"Not Lottie," said Branham. "Lot. He's an old-time Bible fella. You're like Lot's wife."

"Lot's wife is the one got changed to salt. You're thinking of Abraham's wife," said Ezrie, a note of frustration creeping into his voice.

"No, I ain't, dammit," said Branham. "We might look it up in our *Bible.*"

With just a little too much force.

Just a little too much anger.

Hoping Ezrie would catch on.

"Well, if you want to be wrong," said Ezrie, "just go ahead and be wrong. I always said you were too busy sleeping during church to pay much attention. Or too busy making cow-eyes at the girls."

Ezrie's face said that he caught on.

55

Greta's cheeks spread out into a wide smile. "Cow-eyes, Deputy?" She batted her eyelashes at Ezrie. "Tell me more about the Deputy's naughty eyes."

"Sister, the things I could tell you," said Ezrie. "You'd be grateful this old coon dog didn't take you up on your offer."

"That's enough," said Boggs, swinging the gun high.

"I still say it's Lot's wife," said Branham.

"It ain't," said Ezrie.

"Is it?" said Greta.

"I'm ready to shoot the lot of you," said Boggs.

"Alright, alright. Listen," said Branham. "I can prove it. I can prove it."

"And how do you propose to do that?"

"You got a Bible handy?"

Branham held his breath.

"Are you kidding?" said Boggs.

Exhale.

"It just so happens," said Branham. "That my friend and I are carrying a big ol' family Bible in that saddle bag right over there. Now, before you tie us up or kill us, or whatever you plan to do, I'd be obliged if you'd let me look up the passage in question."

"Why should I?" said Boggs.

"Oh, it'll be fun," said Greta. "Let him look."

Boggs eyed the saddle bag.

"I'll look it up myself."

"Like you can read," said Greta, scoffing. "He really can't read a word," she told Branham.

Boggs looked from Branham to Ezrie to Greta. Then back to Branham.

"All right. But be quick about it."

Branham walked deliberately to the side of his horse. "Don't worry about that," he said.

He put his hand on the top of the big book, its gold-lined pages reflecting sunlight onto his fingers.

"I'll be real quick."

And just like that, the book was out of the saddle bag and open and falling.

In his hand was a big Colt .45. It boomed once.

Boggs clutched his arm and his own gun fell to the ground.

"Thus sayeth the Lawd," said Ezrie with a cackle.

The book lay open in the grass. But it wasn't a book. It was a box that looked like a book, with a big hollow square cut from its center. A space big enough to conceal the gun Branham used.

"That ain't no Bible," said Greta.

"That ain't no Shakespeare, neither," said Ezrie.

Branham held the gun up for his friend to see.

"Here's the heirloom, Ezrie."

"I guess it wasn't as heavy I thought."

"For my yoke is easy, and my burden is light," said Branham.

"What's that? A Bible verse? That ain't no Bible verse."

Branham grinned. "It is."

"Is not."

"Will you two shut up?" said Greta.

"I say it is," said Branham.

And arguing about it, they carried their prisoners back to town.

COLLECTING SEAMUS O'SHAUGHNESSY

Having barely survived a tepid spell of schooling in Lincoln, young Bailey Atkins convalesced under the tutelage of Moses Kinkaid in O'Neill and, after acquiring a literal and figurative warbag of funds and favors, hoisted his own Nebraska solicitor's shingle in Gilbert, just a few miles shy of the Niobrara River.

No housekeeper he, the hardwood office entryway was soon patinaed with a dry varnish of dust. Bailey couldn't help but notice the absence of footprints therein.

Business wasn't exactly booming.

But something was.

The morning of May 23 dawned like any other on the open prairie, except for the explosion that roused Bailey from his low-slung office cot, sending him fast to the tall plate glass window where one Willis O'Shaughnessy had painted Bailey's name and occupation in a flowing ivory script for all of Gilbert to see.

From the inside, the window sign was backwards, as was the spectacle greeting Bailey's blurry eyes that morning.

He reached for his glasses, but they didn't help.

In the dusty street outside, Mayor — and sometimes marshal — Clarence Keyes was mounted high on his chestnut mare, dressed in a leather gunbelt and chaps, a Stoeger shotgun bobbing wildly in his hands as he barked orders at a less-than-enthusiastic gaggle of saloon riff-raff, equally armed, but all on foot.

Keyes triggered another explosion from the shotgun.

"Today we ride for the women and children of Gilbert," said Keyes, the chestnut rearing back on her hooves just for show. "For the honor of Seamus O'Shaughnessy!"

It wasn't clear what the six men in the posse would be riding other than broken shoe leather.

That Keyes could suggest that the drunks and ruffians he addressed represented any kind of morality betrayed the desperation of his mysterious cause. That he invoked the sacred name of Gilbert's founder showed he was deadly serious.

Seamus O'Shaughnessy was not a name

anybody in Gilbert took lightly.

Bailey decided to see what was the matter.

He'd slept in his dress cotton shirt and gray wool trousers beside his heavy iron combination safe, it's man-sized height and great depth providing a measure of privacy, so it was simply a matter of slipping into his lace-up leather shoes. After finding only one, and not wanting the war party to charge out of town without explanation, Bailey hopped outside.

"Hello the mayor," he called, leaving the boardwalk to step gingerly across the dusty street. "What goes on here?"

"Look who's up and awake," said Keyes, stroking his heavy red mustache with a gloved hand. "It's a tad early for ye, ain't it, lawyer Atkins?"

Bailey had no idea what time it was, but the hard citrus ball of sun on the horizon was more than halved. "It's not so early," he said through a gaping yawn, knowing Keyes was showing off.

"Aye and it don't have to be too early to collect those gypsies one by one," said Keyes, "haul 'em in to the hoosegow or fill their backsides full of buckshot." Keyes grinned. "Their choice."

Ever since Bailey, a German Lutheran,

61

had moved to town Keyes took every chance he got to point out the solicitor's cultural deficiencies and razz him for not being Irish enough, a serious inditement as far as the sheriff was concerned.

There was only one thing Keyes hated worse than German Lutherans.

"Gypsies?" said Bailey.

"Tis that J. T. Mullen again, and his scurvy band of wagons."

Of course.

The caravan of four colorfully decorated wagons had been making its way along the river for several weeks.

"Let me get my shoe, and I'll join you," Bailey told the assemblage.

At the suggestion, two of the posse deflated to their backsides, and one unbuttoned his shirt collar. "Gonna be a hot one, today," he opined with slurred speech.

Without constant watering from their leader, the followers were wilting in daylight.

"I've got a better idea," Bailey told the mayor. "Let's just you and me visit Mullen's camp." He hooked a thumb over his shoulder. "Should anything untoward happen, we can always call in these fine reinforcements."

Keyes chewed his bottom lip, directing his gaze at the lawyer, then to the motley bunch of sleepy loafers, then back. Finally, he agreed.

"I'll give you five minutes to mount up," he said, turning the mare toward the south end of main street. "I'll be waiting."

It didn't take Bailey long to find his other shoe and scurry across the street to the livery barn where he tossed a saddle onto his loyal old palomino gelding. Seated firmly with reins in hand, he pointed his horse in the direction of the Running Water and Mullen's most likely camping spot along the riverbank. At the edge of town, Keyes joined him.

They galloped nearly a mile through fields of mixed grass and pink blossoming beard-tongue, while meadowlarks darted through the sage-spiced air. A red fox coming in late to its den crossed their path as they crested the final slope, and Bailey congratulated himself on his guesswork. Mullin's camp was exactly where he'd expected it would be, nested casually at water's edge among small springs of cedar and young cottonwood trees.

Before their descent, Keyes reined up close. "You're not armed, are you, son?"

Bailey admitted he was not.

"Take my Bessie, here," said the mayor, holding out the Stoeger.

"I'll take my chances with friendly conversation," said Bailey. "What are we hoping to accomplish anyway?"

"Accomplish?"

"What's the point of this raid?"

"The point? The point is to fight the good fight. Confront the heathens in their den of iniquity."

"Why?"

"Why?" said Keyes.

It was a simple question. One that Bailey didn't think worth repeating, but he did raise an eyebrow.

"Why, because," said Keyes. "It's not proper them being *here*, peddling their cheap shows and awful entertainments. It's not *right.*"

"*Here,*" said Bailey, getting a glimpse at concerns that went beyond the mayor's racial and religious prejudice. "Where exactly do you mean when you say *here*?"

Still holding the scattergun, Keyes flung his arm to the right in a wide ranging arc. "Here. This valley. Where else? The site of *the battle.*"

He closed one eye to the sun and squinted at Bailey over his saddlehorn. "The first battle of Dragonfly Branch," he said like he was talking to a schoolboy. "The cattleman's fight against the sheep men . . . where Seamus O'Shaughnessy met his untimely end nearly two decades ago."

Bailey turned from left to right, studying the arid landscape, realizing that though he knew the story of the old founder's end, he had never made the connection with this particular piece of ground.

"Well then," he told Keyes, "we should have a word with Mr. Mullen."

There was nothing else to do.

Keyes nodded and spun his chestnut in a whirl of dust.

As it turned out, J. T. Mullen was as Irish as Clarence Keyes and canny as Buffalo Bill Cody, though he wore his salt and paprika hair in a more distinguished style than either of those two gents. Dressed in a dandy's black hammer claw jacket and dark pants with a brown cavalry-style hat, Mullen carried himself forward with haughty dignity as Bailey and the mayor approached the row of canvas-enclosed wagons. Halfway there, Mullen raised his hand in greeting.

Bailey's palomino stopped two paces behind the mayor's horse.

"Top of the morning, friends," said Mullen. "Would ye care for a spot of coffee?"

Bailey noted the wisp of smoke coming up in a wavy column behind one of the wagons. Breakfast was his favorite meal of the day, and he'd missed it. The smell of fresh-boiled grounds, cooked eggs, and frying bacon had his stomach rumbling. He opened his mouth to accept the invitation.

"No thanks," said Keyes. "What do you mean camping out here like this?"

Bailey tried not to feel glum.

Instead, he took up the line of questioning before Keyes could continue.

"That is," he said. "Are you just passing through, or are you planning to open for business?"

With a knobby knuckle to his chin, Mullen appeared to ponder the question.

Finally, he spoke. "I ain't rightly sure, yet."

This wasn't the answer Keyes was looking for, but before he could lift the Stoeger, Bailey intervened.

"Out of curiosity, when might you make a decision?"

"You boys ever seen the Bog-man of Uumba-Wells?" said Mullen.

"I don't believe I have," said Bailey. Keyes likewise indicated he had not.

"It's only one of the natural oddities and scientific astonishments housed in my humble train," said Mullen, crooking a finger in Bailey's direction. "Follow me," he said.

Keyes wasn't too enthusiastic, but Bailey

coaxed him along.

Soon the two men were afoot, their horses hobbled on a patch of chewy turf, their attention drawn to a fascinating spectrum of peculiar exhibits.

The plump Mrs. Mullen supplied a pan of Danish abelskievers.

With great aplomb, J. T. Mullen lectured on the unlikely science behind a miniature lightning rod that shot jagged blue bolts through the air.

His wife poured coffee for Bailey and Keyes.

With rapier wit, Mullen uncovered a collection of shark's teeth, showed off a solid gold chamber pot from ancient Egypt, and performed an uncanny jig while exhaling through an Oriental snake charmer's flute.

Bailey wasn't overly impressed with the hollowed out gourd, whitewashed bucket, or the pile of polished rocks, but the coffee and pastries were rich and delicious.

"And that gentlemen, is only the beginning," said Mullen as the four approached the back of the biggest wagon. Painted in black lacquer and gold leaf, it sparkled in the morning sun, it's clean white canvas stretched tight over iron hoops, it's tails held secure with leather ties. "Brace yourselves, men," said Mullen. "The Bog-man of

Uumba-Wells."

Mrs. Mullen kindly excused herself.

"Behold," said Mullen, reaching for a free leather lace.

The back of the wagon billowed open to reveal the hideous masterpiece.

That's exactly what it was, thought Bailey, a masterpiece of plaster of Paris and chicken wire.

The twisted figure of the Bog-man stood six feet tall and brought to mind the Renaissance drawings of emaciated cadavers Bailey had seen in school books. It wore mummified scraps of wool, and its eyes were made of glass. If it weren't for the smell of horsehair and glue, Bailey might have been taken in like a ten-year-old.

Keyes had seen enough.

Breakfast had softened his demeanor, but not his overall resolve. He shook his head, saying, "I'm sorry, Mullen. I'm going to have to ask you to move on. Your menagerie of deception just isn't the kind of thing God-fearing folks need. Let alone pay hard-earned money to see."

"Deception!" said Mullen.

"Hoax," said Keyes.

"I'm gravely disappointed, sir," said Mullen.

"I expect you'll be packed up and out of

here by noon," said Keyes.

"I'd pay for another cup of coffee," said Bailey.

"You will not," said Mullen. "Hospitality is what separates us from the animals," he said, offering Keyes a withering glance. "I'll get you a second cup."

"No time," said Keyes. "We'd best be on our way." He walked to his horse and cocked his head for Bailey to follow.

"I surely do hate to leave this valley," said Mullen. "The wife and I had only just begun to discover its many treasures."

"Treasures?" said Bailey.

"Aye," said Mullen, reaching into his coat pocket and removing an authentic Sioux arrowhead of pinkish hue. "A bear-point if I've ever seen one. Found right over there, the other side of our campfire."

"I expect you'll find a great many arrowheads around here," said Bailey.

"Nothing new to me," said Keyes, climbing into the saddle.

"Arrowheads, square iron nails, horseshoes," said Mullen.

"Bah," said Keyes.

"And then of course, there's the human spinal column," said Mullen.

"Excuse me?" said Bailey.

Mullen stroked his beard.

"Vertebrate," he said.

"Not an animal," said Bailey. "Bison, perhaps. Or bovine."

"A man," said Mullen. "Found by the wife, back yonder at Dragonfly Branch."

The words hung in the air and even the steady wind paused as if for dramatic effect.

"Seamus O'Shaughnessy," Keyes whispered into the silence.

Bailey had his second cup of coffee.

On the way back to Gilbert, Keyes resembled nothing so much as a steam engine, wheels spinning on rails greased by the discovery of Seamus O' Shaughnessy's backbone. Huffing and chuffing, he ground out ambitious plans with impossible timelines, his enthusiasm stoked by anticipated status.

"History will remember this day, son," he told Bailey when they reined up outside the lawyer's Gilbert office building. "The day that Seamus O'Shaughnessy came home." But then his voice was soft and low. "Remember our plan. Don't say a word to anybody. Until Mullen can locate the rest of our founder's sacred remains, we'll keep the discovery a secret."

"Exactly how much did you pay him to hunt for bones?" said Bailey, recalling the surreptitious passing of bills he'd witnessed before leaving the showman's camp.

"Don't you never mind about that," said Keyes. "No price is too great to bring to rest the soul of Seamus O'Shaughnessy."

"How much?"

"Ten dollars."

"And when we have them all?"

"As I said on the way in, once we have a complete collection of remains, we'll give our patriarch the Christian burial he's long deserved, with a rousing ceremony in the center of town, beneath a towering monument that forever will be gazed upon and revered." Keyes breathed in deep. "We'll have it on Founders Day, the reassembled body of Seamus O'Shaughnessy lying in state, presiding over the entire affair. What a celebration it will be."

Bailey followed Keyes' eyes to the sky but saw nothing but another meadowlark and a swarm of gnats.

The old drunk from before had been right.

It was going to be a hot one.

The first bones came in that afternoon, delivered by the mayor himself.

"That's a clavicle," said Keyes with a satisfied grin, covered in sweat and grime, placing the narrow specimen on Bailey's desk between the inkwell and coal oil lamp. "And this one's the scalpel."

"Scapula," said Bailey, adjusting his glasses to study the remains.

"It pains me to admit it, but you're better at this kind of stuff than me," said Keyes. "Book learnin' kind of stuff."

"Did Mullen bring these in?" said Bailey.

"He did not," said Keyes. "After studying on it over my lunch, I decided to ride back out to the battlefield and search for myself."

"Is this all you found?"

"Well, so far," said Keyes. "We're still looking."

Bailey raised his head and messed with glasses. "You and Mullen?"

"Me and some of the boys."

Bailey waited for a further explanation.

"You know," said Keyes. "The boys from this morning."

"You've got them out there looking for Seamus O'Shaughnessy's remains? What happened to keeping this a secret?"

"Founders Day is July 1. If we're going to have the burial ceremony then, I figured we'd need some help."

Bailey turned his attention back to his desk.

"I suspect we should find somewhere safe to . . . ah, collect these."

"I was thinking your office. Right here,"

said Keyes. "Nobody comes in here much."

"Thank you for the reminder."

"I'm just funning you," said Keyes.

Bailey had to admit, the day's undertaking had produced a new attitude in the mayor.

Maybe it wouldn't hurt to play along.

"Alright," said Bailey. "I'll keep Mr. O'Shaughnessy here, in my back room."

Keyes gave the backroom door behind Bailey's desk a dirty look. "It's not too awful secure, is it?" he said.

"Let's keep him in my safe then, shall we?" said Bailey. He picked up the bones and carried them to the big iron box. After spinning the combination, he grasped the thick handle and lugged open the door. Inside, he put the pieces to rest on a measure of green wool. "Let me know if you find anything else."

"I'll tell the boys you said so," said Keyes.

They came with more an hour later.

An ulna and a radius. "The good right arm of our founder," said the carrier.

Random pieces of metatarsal bones. "The foundation upon which he stood."

Donny O'Hara brought in a hip bone.

Covered in dirt, Lem Jones delivered the patella.

That evening after supper, another ulna

joined its mate inside Bailey's safe.

And just before bedtime, a sod-covered Keyes himself contributed a flat plate of ivory he felt certain was from the occipital region.

All in all, a fine day's work.

But the days that followed saw bigger and better progress.

Sam Welles found the sacrum, and when Joe Sims pooled it with his hip bone, they had a pelvis right there on Bailey's desk.

In the vault it went.

Along with Mrs. Leadbetter's tibia, Mrs. O'Brian's tarsus, and Tom Fellow's mandible.

Little Algot Bruhn rode his stick horse across the street to deliver another scapula.

His school pal, August Finch, pointed spade slung over his shoulder, found five ribs.

Bailey's office was busier than it ever had been.

While keeping a dutiful list of the contributions, making sure to give credit where it was due, he made the friendly acquaintance of more than a dozen new citizens. Three of them arranged to have Bailey review their legal holdings and one asked him to draw up a marriage contract.

Never had Bailey seen the town so alive as

when they were occupied with the dead.

There was no arguing that the project had captured the historic imagination of Gilbert.

Only three days since he and Keyes had received the first relic from, and already they had — by careful reckoning — three dozen bones that once belonged to Seamus O'Shaughnessy.

At this rate, the founder would be reverently assembled well before Founder's Day.

The donations kept coming, and time moved on.

"Here's my contribution to the cause," said J. T. Mullen one evening, his coat looking clean and pressed, his campaign hat tilted at a rakish angle. He counted out ten gold eagles onto Bailey's desk blotter.

"What's this for?" said the lawyer.

"This is the initial payment your Mayor Keyes gave me on the day you rode out to my camp."

"I understood this was in exchange for locating Seamus O'Shaughnessy's remains."

Mullen chuckled, "There hasn't been much time to shop for remains the past couple weeks," he said, "or space either for that matter."

"I don't follow you."

"Since word got out, it's all I can do out there to keep the line moving through my exhibits," said Mullen.

"The searchers keeping you busy are they?"

"Seamus O'Shaughnessy is the greatest draw I could have. Why, I've had to make a run all the way over to O'Neill for coffee and supplies more than once. I may not have earned that ten dollars, but I've made it back ten times over selling refreshments and shovels."

"What did you mean about space?"

"Space?"

"You said there wasn't enough space."

"You ain't been out to the valley lately, have you?"

Bailey agreed that he hadn't.

"Well what the Battle of Dragonfly Branch didn't do way back when to tear up the sod, the good folks of Gilbert are doing now. Armed with shovels and rakes, spades and spoons, they've made more holes than craters on the moon. Fair warning! Don't you go riding a horse out there. She's liable to twist a hoof or crack a leg."

With some whimsey, Bailey imagined the tough sod prairie pock-marked and broken.

But he smiled at the glint of lantern light on the gold before him.

Keyes' great endeavor had been a boon

for everyone.

Only question was how long could it last?

"We have a problem," Bailey told Keyes one beautiful June morning as the sun rose above the distant hills.

The mayor leaned back on the back two legs of the wooden chair opposite Bailey's desk, skeptical.

Ever since the effort to collect Seamus O'Shaughnessy had taken hold, Keyes had made it a priority to stop past Bailey's office at least twice a day for progress reports. The two had discovered a mutual interest in cards and coffee, and they'd gotten into the habit of sharing a cup first thing in the morning, and a hand of gin at night.

Bailey didn't think they were friends, exactly, but who else could he share his concern with?

Keyes would have to find out sooner or later anyway.

"It's not that Mrs. Babbit and her cows in the garden again, is it?" said Keyes. "I've warned her about that broken down fence."

Bailey waved away the question and got right to the point.

"It's about Seamus O'Shaughnessy," he said.

"What about him?" said the mayor, letting the front two legs of his chair hit the floor with a thud.

"About the battle of Dragonfly Branch," said Bailey.

"A glorious day."

"How many men were involved in the skirmish?"

Keyes scratched his head.

"My grandpa used to tell me about it," he said. "There were a host of Fennian sheep men from the old country, and there were a few others like yourself. Germans or Scandahoovians or some such. And then there were about five hundred cow men."

"That sounds like an exaggeration," said Bailey.

"Naturally." Keyes scratched his nose. "Why do you ask?"

"Ted Mack brought in a scapula last night."

"Good, good. What's the problem?"

"It's the seventh one we've received."

Bailey stood and walked to the safe. He spun the knob on the makeshift ossuary and pulled open the door. Bones rolled out onto the rug with a sifting of powder. Bones of all shapes and sizes.

Egg white and tan bones. Bones greying and bleached from the sun.

Some covered in hard red clay, others

smeared with slick, black mud.

They made a racket when they hit the floor not unlike a cupful of gambler's dice.

Keyes leapt to his feet, his eyes wide with accusation. "Have a care, man," he said, but when the dust had settled, he appeared to be puzzled. "I still don't see what's wrong."

"Do you know how many bones make up one adult human skeleton?" said Bailey, not bothering to clean up the mess. He moved toward a door behind his desk. "A little over 200," he said.

He grasped the door knob and opened the adjoining room.

It was filled, almost floor to ceiling, with bones.

Femurs, humerus, and knee parts piled up in one corner. Mandibles, parietals, and skulls lolled against a wall. A great pyramid of ribs dominated the center of the room, and the surrounding space was dominated with hands and feet, tiny metacarpals and metatarsals that carpeted the floor like gravel.

"At last count, Seamus O'Shaughnessy's structure consisted of 12,305 individual parts."

"Well, after all," said Keyes, taking a quick peek over Bailey's shoulder, "he wasn't a small man."

"I dare say he wasn't the size of a livery stable," said Bailey.

"Still and all," said Keyes, "we've made fine progress. If we'd but knit him back together."

"Knit him back together? Like a scarf or sweater?"

"More or less, I suppose."

"This sweater would clothe all of Chimney Rock."

The light was beginning to dawn in Keyes' eyes.

"You're suggesting there's more than one man there? There's other people mixed in with the founder?"

"That's a good possibility," said Bailey. "Along with a fair share of coyote, possum, racoon, and fox."

"You know," said Keyes, falling back into his chair, "there's a chance that we don't have the founder here at all."

"That too, is a possibility."

"What are we going to do?"

"I'll tell you what we're going to do. We're going to haul all of these remains back to the river and wash our hands of this ghoulish business," said Bailey.

Keyes scrunched up his features in a sour face. "That seems almost sacreligious."

"As compared to stacking them like cordwood in my storage room?"

"What about the townfolk? After all the work they've done? After the way this thing has brought everybody together? They're expecting the body of Seamus O'Shaughnessy. I promised it would lie in state in the center of town before burial on Founder's Day." Keyes let his shoulders slump. "Can't you rig something together out of all this?"

"Frankenstein himself couldn't rig something together out of this mess."

"That's it! A doctor! We'll call in Doc Snow from O'Neill."

"Do that and we'll be the laughingstock of the state," said Bailey. "If ever there was a blabbermouth, it was Hiram Snow."

"You're right. You're right." Keyes pounded his fist. "But if not a doctor, then who?"

Bailey had to admit he was equally stumped. Carried away with patriotic fervor, everybody in town wanted a piece of the action. Enthused by the new influx of business, Bailey had lost track of his inventory.

Now he thought about the piles of bones in his back room, the collection in his safe. He'd need ten wagons to haul away what had come in piecemeal over a series of weeks.

He'd need a wagon train.

A caravan.

Yes, indeed. A caravan.

"I might have an idea," said Bailey. He opened a side drawer on his desk where Mullen's ten gold coins lay undisturbed.

"How much money do you have on hand?" he asked Keyes.

That year, the Gilbert Founder's Day celebration went off without a hitch.

The Lutherans rolled a pump organ out to the street where Mrs. Leadbetter played several rousing anthems.

The Catholics roasted a pig and supplied young and old alike with mouthwatering pies, cakes and confections.

Mayor Clarence Keyes wrote a poem to honor the town fathers and Bailey Atkins presented a copper plaque that would be affixed to a soapstone monument, marking the grave of the founder.

And if Seamus O'Shaughnessy, resting at ease in an upholstered coffin in the center of town, bore a slight resemblance to the Bog-man of Uumba-Wells with a fresh coat of whitewash, nobody said a word.

Storm Damage

Eddie Lester, on the wagon bench next to his grandpa, watched the river frantically climb. The swirling, foaming current shoved sticks and chaff and sycamore tree boughs past them. Boughs that looked like sea monsters darting their long snaky necks in and out of the waves. Green swells and darker brown undertows reached out, inches away from pulling them down.

And under.

"Steady, boy."

Breathing in the wet smells of the morning's storm, Eddie thought Grandpa was talking to him. But he meant Plugnut, the sorrel gelding hitched to the wagon.

Plugnut whinnied, but Eddie tried to take Grandpa's advice too, tried to steady his nerves.

Together, they looked at the sky.

"Storm's done. Sun'll be out soon."

It wasn't the storm that spooked him,

passing through as it did with rain and wind and thunder that had snapped him awake that morning like an electric switch.

Storms blew in, but they always blew out.

Storms weren't anything permanent.

"They say you can never step into the same river twice," said Grandpa. "You ever heard that one?"

Eddie shook his head.

He didn't want to look at the river anymore.

He didn't want to think about it.

He'd lived his whole life here on the banks of the Moreau. He'd seen it spiteful enough to flood Grandpa's corn.

Angry enough to uproot trees.

He'd never seen it go completely mad.

Yesterday, a solid oak bridge spanned the water, from the spot where they waited, to Cedar Grove, across the way.

Today, the bridge was gone, vanished, the space ahead filled only with the triumphant rushing and roaring of water.

In a world where things could change, the bridge had been unchanging.

In a life of ups and downs, the bridge was straight and true.

Now, it was splinters . . . tumbling downstream.

Grandpa simply said, "We'll have to go

around."

When he moved the wagon back, sent Plugnut along a parallel path, then away from the river at an angle, Eddie breathed a sigh of relief.

The clouds were parting when they crossed the hill at Parker's Mill.

"Knew a girl once, a long time ago," said Grandpa. "A long time before grandma. She was the kind of girl who called you chicken, you didn't do certain things with her."

Eddie saw Mrs. Parker in her long apron, outside tossing a forkful of hay to her cows. A couple of broken maple tree branches sprawled across her lawn. He waved, but she didn't see him.

"This girl met me one night at a dance. Asked if I wanted to take a ride in her dad's wagon. A wagon a lot like this one."

Eddie pretended to listen, but he was more interested in seeing the storm damage. It looked like the Johnson farm had lost a barn roof.

"I wasn't about to be called no chicken. So we went for a ride under the stars, this hellcat and me," said Grandpa. "She was the most beautiful girl I'd ever seen."

When Grandpa stopped talking, Eddie turned to look at him. Grandpa's face was folded with age and spackled with a random growth of whiskers. The puffy, gray eyes looked down on him. "Do you understand what I'm saying, Eddie?"

"I suppose," said Eddie, not understanding at all. He turned back to the torn landscape around them.

Eddie supposed they were lucky at their little house, Grandpa and Grandma and him. The potato cellar flooded a bit, and they'd lost some limbs off trees, but nothing like the damage out here in the open country.

Who could have imagined they'd be better off so close to the river?

"So . . . I saw this girl a month or so later, again at a dance."

"What was her name?" said Eddie, just to prove he was paying attention.

The Johnson's barn was a complete disaster. In memory, it stood two stories high, painted red with a peaked shingle roof. Now, it was an open husk, like a bursting shell had gone off inside, and the smell of moldy hay and horse manure filled the air.

"Whose name?"

"This girl you're talking about."

"Thelma."

Grandpa started again. "So I see this girl at a polka dance. She comes out from behind this big accordion player and tells me she's late."

Several men were already cleaning up debris around the barn. Eddie waved. This time, somebody saw him and waved back.

"I don't know what she's talking about, 'late.' So I say, 'Am I late for the dance?' She meant a different kind of 'late.' Thelma meant she was late for her monthly. She asked me what I was going to do about it."

The road curved down away from the Johnsons' and, looking across the river valley, Eddie could easily see the path of the storm.

Layers of torn sod, trees bent and pitched at a variety of odd angles. It was all quite exciting.

Grandpa turned back toward the river, toward the crossing at Jewel's Ford, and Eddie's stomach fluttered.

"Right then and there, I told Thelma I didn't want to see her again. But that was a lie. I did want to see her again. But I also knew she was the kind of girl would lie to boys just to get 'em into trouble." Grandpa shook his head and whistled at Plugnut as they rolled along down the hill. Through a line of trees, Eddie could see the river, could smell the brine and raw dirt.

"I spent every day of my life wanting to see Thelma again. Wondering what happened to her."

"What if Jewel's Ford is washed out too?" said Eddie.

"It won't be," said Grandpa.

Eddie took his word for it. Grandpa had lived here a long time. He'd seen storms come and go.

"Is this the worst storm you've ever seen?" Eddie asked.

Grandpa nodded. "It could be, at that," he said. "I suppose we were due."

But somehow, Eddie didn't think they were talking about the same thing.

At Jewel's Ford, the water lapped at the underside of the iron bridge, and big piles of wood and garbage clung to the railings where the current kept stashing it.

Plugnut stepped onto the oak planks and the bridge shuddered.

"Your grandma never heard that story. Not until this morning."

Eddie didn't like the way the river looked. He didn't like the way the bridge creaked and groaned.

Neither did Plugnut.

"Maybe just wait until tomorrow to go to town?" said Eddie.

"Can't wait any more," said Grandpa.

Eddie was surprised when he handed over the reins and stood up.

"Where are you going?"

"S'pect this is far enough. No need for you to wait."

"Wait?"

"You can turn around, take the wagon back home."

Eddie blinked his eyes and watched Grandpa climb to the ground. Across the bridge, on the opposite bank, another wagon waited.

A strange woman sat on the bench.

"Don't you worry about me, son," said Grandpa. "The clouds are going away. The sun'll be out soon."

Eddie watched Grandpa walk across the bridge, then his pace quickened to a trot.

He watched him climb into the other wagon.

At the last moment, Eddie waved his hand, tried to call out.

But the other wagon was already gone.

After a while, Eddie took Plugnut back the way they came.

At the Johnson place, he stopped to help pick up after the storm.

THE BETTER SALESMAN

After putting off the job until late May, Anderson Teague went hunting one morning for his long-handled grubbing hoe in the iron pile behind his two-room shack. There was no more arguing with the patch of thistles growing up around his front door.

Something had to give.

Teague just hoped it wasn't his back when he dug out the noxious weeds.

Then again, after three years on the claim, he was getting used to hard work.

It hadn't always been this way. For more years than he cared to count, the worst his back went through was a day's ride on his old buckboard wagon under the hand-painted wood sign: The Better Salesman.

That's what they called him in those days.

Kicking at a tangle of lightning rods and cable, turning over a kettle of rusted square nails, he found the hoe half-buried in the Wyoming sod, overgrown with new grass.

Almost everything in the pile was overgrown, from horseshoes and band saw blades to rolls of barbed wire and broken lengths of angled scrap. Inventory from a past life.

If it was made of metal, Teague sold it, swapped it, or sat on it.

He swung the hoe high into the air and the cast iron head flew off its rotted wood handle to land with a thud and poof of red dust.

The last few years had seen a lot more sitting than selling.

Teague dropped the handle and swiped at the sweat on his stubbled cheeks, rubbed the dusty, dry smell of sagebrush from his nose, and turned back to the pile of debris.

A worthless collection if ever there was one.

The leftovers from one storm-wracked venture after another.

The peddler's peddler, just a little too clever, a little too quick with a sweet little deal, Teague had dealt well, but not well enough. Now he stood penniless on his granddad's old claim, digging around the remains of his many past lives.

Nails, saw blades, and lightning rods. Sun-browned and worthless.

Just like Anderson Teague.

Summer wind whistled through the empty stalls of the sagging two-story pole barn west of the shack, and the hay mow door banged open, then closed. His grandad built the barn in '79, adding the shack as an afterthought, a nod to a man's need for a bed when tending horses in the high-country.

The old man had been gone a long time, and there never were many horses.

Around front, Shep started barking, and Teague turned to peer down the prairie road.

Who could be passing by so early in the day?

Following two swayback roans, a high-wheeled Conestoga-style wagon rolled off the plains into Teague's front yard, its contents hidden by its eggshell-white canvas. Two men crouched on the wagon's rigid front bench. One held the swaybacks' reins and wore vested city clothes with a black bowler derby. The other one, younger and heavier, was dressed in a sloppy long shirt and denim pants with holes at the knees.

Teague's throat tightened at the heavy smell of kerosene surrounding the rig.

He adjusted his floppy, sweat-stained hat, then picked up the handle of the grubbing hoe just for something to carry around the side of the shack. Something to show the men he meant business if they got too pushy.

Teague grinned to himself. He sorta hoped they would.

The wagon came to a stop twenty feet from the front door. The sign painted on the high canvas side said "Max Plank and Son, Painters."

Shep circled the rig, yapping like he had a rabbit in its hole.

"How do?" said the man closest to Teague, doffing his little round hat.

Max Plank.

"Good afternoon to you, sir," said the shabby other.

The son.

"That's a mighty fine dog you got there. Border collie, ain't she?"

Shep continued trotting around, a wide smile on her face.

Teague held on to the hoe. "Turn your wagon around and head out the way you came in."

"A moment of your time, sir."

"I don't think so."

"A drink of fresh water."

"You wouldn't deny us a drink on a hot morning?" said the son.

"I guess I would." Teague took a step

93

forward, shooing the horses with the wood handle. "Git. Git." Sniffing, he rubbed his nose again. He'd known barn painters before, even helped a few out.

None of 'em ever had such a stink as these Plank boys.

Shep sneezed, then added a few barks of disgust.

"Now that's a magnificent structure," said Max Plank, standing up from the wagon bench to face the barn.

"Hell of a barn," said the son.

"You ever see such workmanship?"

"I ain't never seen it, Daddy."

Max gave a series of drawn out humble nods. He turned to Teague.

"If I might just ask before we leave? Who raised that splendid edifice?"

"Who built the barn ain't none of your business," said Teague with a heavy sigh. "Who's talking to you is. I said move along."

The painters continued to ignore him.

"Cherry Tree Red?" said Max. "Bright and shining, a blossom on the horizon, a scarlet beacon of cheer."

"With snow white trim," said the son. "Cold and delicious."

"Like iced cream," said Max.

"I don't care to have my barn painted," said Teague.

"It would be a challenge," Max told his son.

"But what a showpiece. Folks would talk. Word would spread. Our reputation . . ."

"Would be assured in these parts." Max stroked his chin. "Could we do it for half price?"

"Don't see why we couldn't."

Max Plank looked down at Teague. "You heard my boy. We'll give you half-off our normal rates."

"Half-off my ass."

Teague knew how it worked. These boys pulled in, promising to do a job in a few days, then hung around for weeks to free-load grub and any other handout they could get.

He'd done it himself a time or two. A lot of 'em stayed drunk half the time, drinking their own watered-down paint thinner.

It had never got that bad for Teague. At least not yet.

Shep sneezed again.

Max Plank's eyes were red rimmed and sliding back and forth, from Teague to the barn, and back again. He licked his chapped lips and picked at his trousers. "We can have it done in three hours," he said.

Teague blinked into the sun, the wagon shimmering out of focus.

"Three hours?"

"Less time than that if we get started now, before the worst of the heat."

Teague balled up his fists and planted them on his hips.

Here was something new.

"Just how do you propose to finish a job that size in three hours?" He laughed out loud. "There's no way in hell. Unless you got twelve men huddled up in the back of that wagon. That's a three- or four-day job. Minimum."

"A four-day job for you and me in our youth," said Max, eager to explain.

"This here's the 20th century," said the son.

"How about you show him, boy?"

The fat kid jumped to the ground.

Teague wasn't about to let these devils trip him up. There was no way they were laying one damn brushstroke to so much as a single stick of grass.

But they'd accomplished one thing. They'd stoked his curiosity.

He supposed it wouldn't hurt to take a look at the back of the wagon.

With Shep at his heels, and still swinging the hoe handle, Teague followed Max Plank's son to the rear of the Conestoga.

Once there, Max appeared around the

other side and together the two salesmen pulled open the canvas to reveal the contents of the wagon.

"The 20th Century, sir," said Max.

Without trying to hide it, Teague smiled.

There, mounted on a heavy plate of iron, bolted to the wagon's reinforced oak floor, before three rusted iron barrels, was a small gasoline engine and pump-jack with a seemingly endless roll of rubber hose attached.

"Let me tell you how it works," said Max.

"Oh, I get it," said Teague.

"We don't use brushwork," said the son. "The paint is sprayed on. With the pump."

"Don't you see?" said Max. "This little marvel provides better coverage in a fraction of the time."

"I told you, I understand."

"Twenty-five dollars," said Max. "That's for two colors. Red and white."

Teague knew painters who would charge twice that much.

"You spray the white trim too?"

"You'd be surprised at the precision of the nozzle on that hose."

"Three hours?"

"Three hours or less," said the son.

"Or you don't pay us," said Max.

"I may not pay you, anyway," said Teague.

"Your satisfaction is our guarantee."

While the three men stood looking at the engine, inhaling smells of gas, paint, and kerosene, Teague surprised himself by actually considering the offer.

Maybe the fumes were getting to him.

But he was already thinking about the future. Some long dormant part of him was alive and cooking up a sweet little deal for himself.

Paint the barn today, maybe do the house someday by himself.

Then fix up a few things. Put some new hinges on that hay mow door.

He might actually unload the place and have bankroll enough to go somewhere else.

Try something new.

The whole thing could start now, today. If only he really were the better salesman.

"There's just one problem," said Teague, "I don't think you can do it in the time you said. Not to my satisfaction."

Max did an adequate job of looking hurt. "Are you calling us liars, sir?"

"I'm calling it like I see it," said Teague. "You may as well know, I'm no stranger to your trade. There's a lot of preparation work here. Hose to unroll. Motor to get working."

He exaggerated a slow head shake.

The son tossed out a new offer. "Say two

and a half hours."

"Two and a half hours." Teague chewed his lip. "Now that might be worth the money." He spread out upturned hands. "But plain and simple, I don't believe you can do it."

Max Plank's eyes flared wide at the challenge. He reached into his coat and Teague stepped back.

The painter brought out a tarnished pocket watch.

"Say the word, and we'll get to work." He handed Teague the timepiece.

Now it was Teague's turn to raise his eyebrows. "I'm gonna go pull a jug of water from my well and sit down there by my iron pile. You boys got two hours and thirty minutes." He looked at the watch. "Starting now."

The gas popper made a hell of a racket, and if the kerosene stink was bad before they started, it was three times worse now.

Twice in a half hour Teague had turned his back on the entire enterprise to walk out across the open range and suck in lungfuls of fresh air. He stood nearly a quarter mile away from the claim and looked back. Shep circled around, poking her nose into prairie dog holes.

The painters were working steady along the side of the barn in a swirling cloud of red mist. Max was stripped down to shirt and trousers, leaving his vest, coat, and derby on the seat of the wagon. The boy had tossed his shirt aside and his puffy soft skin was a blazing pink, equal parts sunburn and paint.

"What a damned mess," Teague said out loud and Shep sneezed in agreement.

"Hell of a way to make a living," he said.

The thing of it was, they were making good progress. They'd started on the northeast side and were working their way around the barn clockwise.

Teague looked at the pocket watch. After forty-five minutes, the Planks were almost half done, the bleached, dry barn wood sucking up the paint like a thirsty blood tick.

Satisfaction guaranteed, the old man had said.

Well, no matter how good a job they did, the rifle inside Teague's back door wasn't about to be satisfied with the job. Paying the Planks wasn't a part of Teague's home improvement plan.

The breeze kicked up a thick whiff of kerosene: the secret of the Plank's speed and their ability to cut costs. Every barn painter Teague ever knew cut his paint with thinner, but the Planks' setup was the worst ever. The stuff chugging through the pump and landing on the barn wall contained less paint than a bargirl's lipstick. Even from a distance, Teague could see the gunk running in long, sloppy curves down the boards.

It was the kind of sloppy work that would make his refusal to pay more honest than he'd figured.

He slapped the pocket watch shut and, walking toward the iron pile, breathed in and out through his mouth.

Next time Teague opened the lid, Max Plank was walking toward him, wiping his scarlet hands on a dirty gray rag. Teague leaned back in a wood rocker beside the iron pile, the watch in one hand, a rifle flat across his lap. He returned the painter's smug grin.

"Glory be, that sun is a booger," said Max. "But I believe we got her licked."

"That so?"

"It'll take an hour or two to dry. Not long in this weather."

Teague chuckled. "That stuff you call paint was dry the minute it hit the barn."

"Barn wood does soak up the pigment."

"Soaks up the kerosene. Don't know how much paint you actually used."

Unfazed by the comment, Max dabbed at

coat of pink covering his neck, cheeks and forehead. The barn's hay mow door banged open, then closed and both men turned to watch the son work at rolling up the wet, stained paint hose.

Once a sun-bleached cool gray, the two-story building was now a brownish rust color with fuzzy pink outlines, swirling mirage-like in a field of shimmering hot fumes. Teague peered through squinty lids and watched the kid toss down the hose and dig into his pants pocket.

"If I may, I'd like to ask you for the time," said Max, extending his hand.

Teague tossed him the watch. "Oh, you made the deadline, alright," he said. "With ten minutes to spare."

At the barn, the son was rolling a cigarette with papers and a sack of tobacco.

"I'm glad to hear it," said Max. "We'll just get everything cleaned up and then I'll be back over to settle up."

"Ain't gonna be no settlin' up." Teague put both hands on the rifle. "Like I told you before, you can turn your wagon around and come back the way you came."

"Beg your pardon?"

"You heard me."

"We had a deal, sir."

"Yes, we did. Satisfaction guaranteed, you

said. Well, I ain't satisfied."

"I don't understand." Max Plank flung an outstretched arm toward the barn. "That's a damned fine job for what you're paying."

"You didn't hear me. I ain't paying."

Max opened his mouth, then closed it before anything came out.

Oddly enough, the kid was still standing by the barn, unlit cigarette in hand. Like he was waiting for something.

"This ain't my first rodeo, Mr. Plank. Matter of fact, I used to be something of a wheeler dealer just like yourself. They called me The Better Salesman."

Max narrowed his eyes, turned to look at the boy.

"Then they called you wrong, sir."

Max nodded.

The kid tossed the cigarette to the ground. Brought up his other hand. Lifted his left foot.

Too late, Teague realized what he was going to do.

A match blazed to life on the son's boot heel.

"Like you observed," said Max, the better salesman. "Lot of kerosene there."

Teague closed his eyes and gripped the rifle with white-knuckled frustration.

He should've seen it coming. Should've

known there'd be an angle. There was always an angle.

Shep barked, and Teague's mind went to the iron pile.

The sawblades, the cables, the lightning rods.

"I'll pay, I'll pay," said Teague, tossing his rifle aside and rising to his feet.

Max smiled and waved at his son who promptly ground the sputtering match into the dirt.

"I knew you'd see reason."

"But before I do, I've got a proposition for you."

"A proposition?"

"Picture this," said Anderson Teague, spreading his hands wide, spinning a yarn long and colorful.

The match Max's son had was nothing more than a spark. A spark could come from anywhere. Out here on the open range, sparks were frequent in the form of lightning.

And who would want their fresh painted barn to get struck by lightning? Especially a barn coated in Max Plank's unique mixture of pigment.

A unique, highly flammable mixture.

Nobody would want that, would they?

So wouldn't the sensible man part with a

few additional dollars for a lightning rod? Maybe two?

"Indeed he might," said Max, seeing the potential. "But where would I find enough lightning rods to make a go of it?"

Teague put his arm around the older man. "Step right this way, my friend."

And just like that, he was back on top. The legend on the sign still belonged to Anderson Teague.

One Last Job

No matter how much booze I poured down, my mouth tasted stale with last night's pinto beans and possum fat.

And I smelled like a latrine.

Felt high as the ground floor. Been feeling that way ever since Paula died.

"What you need is to get back to work, Sheriff. If you don't mind my saying so."

"I do, actually," I told Tabitha, fingering the tin star on my shirt.

"You cleaned up this town real good," said Tabitha. "So quiet lately, I can't hardly believe it."

"So quiet I can't stand it," I said.

I shoved my tin cup across the surface of the polished oak bar. "Fill 'er up."

Tabitha. Big moon pie face with squinty eyes. "We all miss her, Sheriff. But you oughtn't to drink so much in the morning."

"Morning, hell."

But it was. Outside, on the boardwalk,

Barter Gulch came to life. Cattleman hustled along the boardwalk. The rich aroma of coffee and feedstuff drifted over from the mercantile. Old Stu Warner cracked open the doors of the bank next door.

My home. Me and Paula's. Before that damned kicking horse took her.

I couldn't stand it no more.

"I've decided to leave town," I said.

Tabitha looked at me like a sister and poured the drink. Kept her hand tight on the bottle, like she was afraid I might reach across and jerk it away.

"Got one last job to do," I said, gazing into the amber liquor. "Yeah. One job is all I need."

It would be easy, I told myself again.

Nobody but me and Tabitha in the saloon this time of morning.

An even $100 in the till.

In the mirror behind the bar, I watched a horseman ride into Barter Gulch, dust billowing around his steeldust gelding. I tossed back the drink. When Tabitha closed her eyes to sneeze, I plucked the star from my shirt and jammed it into my pants pocket.

Then I put my hand on my gun.

A hundred dollars would take me a long way from Barter Gulch. A long way from the memories.

I pulled my gun from its leather holster. Laid it gently on the bar.

Tabitha's eyes were big as pancakes.

The shot rang out.

I heard her scream at the same time the bottle crashed to the floor.

I whirled around to see two masked horsemen, on steeldust mares like the first rider.

Dismounting to the board walk.

Guns blazing.

One of them shot into the air again and clomped toward the bank.

I picked up my cold gun from the bar.

"You knew something was gonna happen, didn't you, Sheriff?"

I gave Tabitha a big grin.

Then stood up and turned toward the action.

I pinned the star back onto my shirt.

"I'm glad you ain't left town just yet."

Gun held at my side, I started walking toward the trouble next door.

"Me too," I said. "One last job like this is just what I need."

Tell Tail

Sitting safe where you are — reading my words — you may think me mad, and that's your judgement to make.

But I tell you, I'm not to blame for the murder on Mulberry Lane.

How unfair to judge me mad. For truly, I'm more sane now than ever before. Now that I realize the truth about so many things.

The mulberry, for example. As malevolent as it is ubiquitous — and this needs to be recognized.

It's dirty. It stains.

It needs to be held accountable.

The black-hearted juice doesn't simply mar the beige corduroy trousers or white cotton blouse. Oh, no! So, too, does the violet violence sneak into your heart.

I've known it for years, but only with the Mulberry Lane incident did I realize how far the pernicious things would go to inflict their madness.

The humid day was unusually warm for a Missouri June, with an outside temperature more akin to cookstove July.

Dressed in a light shirt and pants already described, I retired from the stifling oven of my wallpapered study to walk with my dog, Solomon, along the trickling river in the yellowing grass at Claysville park.

My brick, two-story home resides on the edge of the place and it's often that I take my leisure there.

A line of wilting day lilies struggled in the long grass, listing to left and right.

Letting the beast run ahead, off his lead, I closed my eyes to the sun and breathed in what little breeze came off the water's surface.

The creek's edge was hard and crumbling, so we stuck to the center of the trail, dappled as it was with sunlight where it swerved under an occasional walnut or elm.

At first our pace was brisk, but I'm afraid heat exhaustion set in to both of us quickly enough. A side path to a mulberry grove seemed a welcome respite.

Entering the shady place, Solomon barked as if in happy greeting.

A mixed breed wrapped in a coat of flowing dark fur, Solomon's mongrel heritage betrays his name.

Wisdom is not his strong suit, and if he were more physically sound, I'd call him Samson.

Because of the long hair.

But Darcy named him Solomon as a pup, and Solomon he is.

He loved Darcy almost as much as me.

And so, he, too, owns a portion of the blame for the day's events.

For just as I first picked up the scent of Darcy's lilac perfume, the same familiar smells must have assaulted his nose.

And so he recognized our old friend, and ran to her.

She stood beneath the row of mulberry trees, the trail doubly stained with spots of dark shadow and the spatter of dropped berries.

But awful as they were, the berries were secondary to the terror inflicted on my mind at that moment.

For here was Darcy.

With a freshly placed ring on that finger which forever barred me from her intimate company.

Why she was there, I don't know. Maybe the life of a pastor's wife was as stifling as the heat of my own wallpapered study. Maybe the afternoon's malaise had driven her out to Claysville Park and the secluded lane in hopes of a moment's excitement.

Perhaps in hopes of a private rendezvous?

In hopes of the heat rekindling old flames?

Did she hope to find me, where I so often stroll?

But even as I closed in on that delicate frame, that lightly powdered porcelain face, those tender lips — she raised a hand to her cheek and a single ray of sunlight stabbed through the trees like a lance to strike that slim band of gold.

The ring! The ring!

Forever it will haunt me.

The sign that another — a man of the cloth, no less — had received the reward for which I had toiled so long, for so many months of air-headed fluff and flattery.

I cast my eyes away, at the ground, just as another mulberry fell from the over-burdened leaves above.

There were scores of berries surrounding both of us. Some whole, some crushed to pulp. Some nothing more than a liquid dark stain in the dirt. Darcy and I stood in a veritable sea of wasted mulberries.

Already one had left its telltale black mark on the toe of my light leather boot.

"I should have to scrub that away," I said to myself.

Darcy must have taken that as a greeting,

for at that moment she deigned to speak.

But the ring was again in my vision as she reached out to me.

And what happened next, I can't — no, won't — describe.

Simply understand that what happened to Darcy was not my fault.

It was the berries, you see.

The berries that stained my fingers as they groped and squeezed.

Berries that fell onto the back of my shirt, my neck, my hair.

That marred my trousers as I knelt under the weight of my task.

And when I was done, the berries covered both myself and Darcy's still husk.

Solomon's bark woke me as if from a dream, and we retired quickly to the study where I appraised my appearance in the tall looking glass there.

Mulberry stains! Black and red!

Blue, indigo, violet. I had become a living palette for some madly depressive painter, each blot a reminder of the vile act I committed. Each stain a confession warranting my own choking death.

I'm afraid I went on something of a tear at that point. Normally tidy and well kept, my study became a clutter of turned over furniture and broken glass works as I raged to find washcloths and cleaning solvents.

Thankfully, Solomon's water dish was dry — I found it afterwards perched on a priceless set of hardbound sonnets that might have been completely ruined.

Initially, I set to work on my shoes, for they were the most discolored.

I scrubbed as if my life depended upon it — for I well knew that it did.

No one must be able to connect me with the grotesque figure in repose at Mulberry Lane.

After the shoes were spotless, I stripped out of my attire and examined every pore, every follicle, every highly evolved cell of my Grecian form, making sure to expunge every hint of the berry blood.

I decided to burn my clothing, and so stuffed shirt and pants into a compact canvas sack. After dressing in an immaculate suit of blazing white, I immediately took the incriminating apparel outside, dumped it in an iron trash barrel behind my home, and set it ablaze.

I entered my study through the back way only to find Samson crying at his overturned water dish, his unrolled tongue like a speckled parchment map.

For it, too, was covered in mulberry stains! And if his tongue, then so too his hair, the pads of his paws!

In my haste to cleanse myself of the afternoon's doings, I had forgotten Solomon's guilt.

And so I set to work.

Brushing, scrubbing with lye, wiping away the color from his ebony hair.

I picked seeds like ticks — that to a trained forensic eye — might give the poor beast away.

Finally, secure in his sanitation, I again saw the lolling, water-starved tongue, its dimpled surface dark with spots.

Damning the elusive nature of the berries, I rose to secure a dipper of water.

When a knock came at the door.

Heavy-handed and sure of purpose.

"Open us, sir," came the voice. "Official business, sir."

Panic!

I made a half-hearted attempt to right a chair I'd tipped over in my rage. Replaced a book to a table.

But there wasn't time.

The knocking became insistent.

I smoothed back my hair.

Appraised both myself and Solomon in the looking glass.

Other than the tongue, I saw nothing that would give us away.

The knocking became a pounding.

"I know you're in there, sir."

Quickly I shut Solomon behind a hallway door that led to my bedroom.

Then, with a deep breath, I opened the front entrance to the familiar face of Constable M_____ framed as it was in muttonchops and a wig of sandy disarray.

"Good afternoon to you," I greeted. "Pray tell, what's this all about?"

"I'm afraid I've got some rather sobering news, sir. Would you mind overly much if I stepped inside?"

"Of course not. Please, come in," I said, the charming host.

As the constable made his way into the study and found a chair, my eyes furiously darted this way and that, alert for any sign of mulberry remnants.

Ever so gradually, I began to breathe at ease.

The room was clean.

I was clean.

Solomon whined behind his closed door.

"It's about a murder, sir."

"Murder? Oh my!"

"I'm afraid it's an acquaintance of yours, sir. A Mrs. Darcy Reynolds."

"Not Darcy!" I said, thrusting my hand to my lips with a flourish.

116

For you see, I performed on the stage as an undergraduate, and this part of my deception didn't worry me in the least.

"Yes, sir. I'm sorry."

Solomon whined again, and I realized he had yet to have a drink.

To his credit, the constable watched closely as I feigned a few tears and let my shoulders shake just enough in light sobbing as to make the fellow feel uncomfortable.

He was simply doing his job.

"It seems to have just happened this afternoon. May I ask where you've been?"

"Of course, of course." I regained my composure and answered straightforwardly. "I've been here all afternoon. Reading."

Solomon pawed at his side of the door and, for the first time, the constable noticed that we weren't alone in the house.

"Your dog, sir?"

"Yes, yes. He sleeps in my bedroom. Better ventilation. The heat's more bearable there you understand."

"I see."

"Well, I just naturally closed the door when you knocked," I said.

The constable raised his eyebrows as Solomon continued to demand his release.

"I wouldn't want him to bother you," I said.

"Wouldn't bother me in the least," said the constable, slapping his knee. "I love a good dog."

"I really should get him some water," I said. "The heat . . ."

"By all means."

As I rose, the next words froze my heart.

"Has the dog also been here all afternoon?"

I turned, holding tight to my calm.

"Why do you ask, sir?"

"No reason. Just wondering if you had let him out at any point?"

"No, no," I carelessly assured him. "Solomon and I have been here together all afternoon."

Fool!

Now what had I done?

If I let Solomon out into the company of the law, the constable will surely note mulberry stains on the dog's tongue.

Which would lead to more questioning.

Perhaps a search in and around the house.

Maybe more questioning about why a suit of clothes might be burned on a hot summer afternoon?

Surely they'd been rendered harmless ash by now?

Or had they?

"Solomon must have his drink," I said and first excused myself to a kitchen area where I slowed my thinking while pumping full a pan of fresh water.

There was nothing to fear.

I would walk into the next room and set down the pan of water.

Then, I'd open the door, releasing poor dehydrated Solomon.

Thirsty as he was, his keen nose would go for the water before visiting the constable.

And the last vestige of mulberry stains would be wiped away.

Again, I told myself, there was nothing to fear.

I carried out the plan flawlessly and reclaimed my chair as Solomon lapped at the water with greed.

"What else can I do for you, Constable?" I asked.

"Beautiful dog," he said.

"Thank you."

Lap, lap, lap.

The sound of Solomon's tongue on the water was music to the ears. Each splash a cleansing acquittal.

"Shame to keep him cooped up in a hot apartment all afternoon."

"As I said, the ventilation in the bedroom

is better."

Still Solomon lapped at his water, drinking it all in, filling his stomach with the cold, life-giving liquid.

Lap, lap, lap.

The sound like a drum, pounding out a rhythm. Like a heartbeat.

"I just think a dog might like a walk through the park."

"No, no. I've been by his side all afternoon. Right here."

"You've been by his side all afternoon."

"That's right."

"I see."

"He rather likes it inside," I said, for it seemed the constable was looking for more.

But I couldn't understand the questioning and was growing more irritated by the second.

Lap, lap, lap.

Hadn't the cur finished his portion yet?

"If that's it then, I'll be on my way."

I watched the man rise from his chair, not trusting myself to stand without a tremble.

Lap, lap, lap.

What was it about that infernal drumming? That obnoxious, overriding sound of Solomon, gorging himself on water, his stomach swelling to the point of —

"Your dog, sir."

The lapping had become a series of halting, gagging grunts.

Standing, I admit to falling against the arm of the chair as I witnessed the dog's involuntary spasms.

Mouth wide, belly convulsing.

"Not to be alarmed," said the constable. "He simply took in too much water at too fast a rate. He'll be fine in a moment."

And with that, Solomon gave up the contents of his stomach.

"Villain!" I shouted. "I admit the deed! Here, here! The mulberries!"

And I was forever lost in an acrimonious sea of black and red and violet and blue as a recognizable, barely digested fount spilled out at the constable's feet.

Ida Tully and the Telephone

Thirty-four years a bachelor, Marvin Dell rubbed his woolen sock feet together, warming them at the fat-bellied cookstove in the ranch house corner, and pulled a match from the center pocket of his overalls.

Flame at the open grate cast flickering shadows over the unfinished walls of the line shack and its few sticks of furniture. Weird silhouettes of Marvin in his rocker and his younger brother Emil, his relentless jaw working over the cherrywood telephone monster.

"I've got the whole night here," said Emil, his left hand gently stroking the transmitter arm, his right cradling the receiver soft against his ear.

"I love-oo, too, Cookie-nose," he said.

Things between 22-year-old Emil Dell and his girl, Ida Tully, were *just that serious.*

Marvin struck the match with his thumbnail, then spun a cigar through the flame, sucking smoke, smacking his lips.

Emil slapped a hand over the telephone mouthpiece. "Hush!" he said. "Hush! Can't you see I'm on the phone with I-daaaa?"

Marvin closed his eyes and wondered how it had come to this.

Only four months since his boss installed the telephone in the cabin, the line stretching across the telegraph poles along the Niobrara River, connecting the farthest acres of the Bar-Seven ranch to the main house and the village of Albertson where Ida lived.

Four months of slow torture.

But wasn't it a blessing for the community?

Only a week after installation, didn't the phone save a Bar-Seven haybarn from fire? Didn't it save young Billy Carson's life a week later when he was snake-bit and the village doc was immediately called in?

Marvin deliberated while chewing the end of his cigar.

To be honest, he'd never really liked the Carson kid.

"No, no," said Emil back at the phone. "I'm all alone here. Except for Maarr-viinnn, of course."

And this habit of stretching out names.

Emil had picked up the affectation from Ida.

From their endless conversations on the telephone.

Marvin smoked and eyed his Colt .45 hanging beside the cabin's front door.

One more stretched out name and Eeeee-mil might pick up a bullet.

"Drinking coffee," said Emil. "Rest assured, I never touch anything stronger. You know where drunkards end up."

Marvin nodded to himself, sucking in apple-flavored smoke.

Drunkards.

Yes, indeed.

That first week, Emil took to the telephone like Uncle Willy took to hard liquor in '02, not bothering to start with short nips and shots, but going straight for the heavy dosage.

Ida was the same way apparently.

Suddenly, she was there at the end of the wire, like she came installed with the damn thing.

Instead of riding fences, finding lost calves, fixing up the front porch, Emil spent hours out of each day hanging onto the box, his face pressed against it, his arms wrapped around it, worshipping it like it was a newborn calf at the udder.

"Yes, well you knooooww how obstinate Marvin can be."

Marvin rocked back and forth.

The hell of it was, calves got weaned, Uncle Willy turned yellow and died, but Emil prospered.

Thriving on the daily dose of battery-driven static and Ida's noisy gabbing, he was more content than ever, his orange mop of hair growing thick and long, his skin rosy and flush.

Since the end of summer, the boy had put on fifteen pounds.

"Ha! Ha-ha-haaaaaahhhh!"

And developed an ungodly cackle.

The wet end of Marvin's cigar was in creamy shreds.

With warm feet but frayed nerves, and winter just on the horizon, Marvin decided to do something about his predicament.

"We got all winter to talk," Emil said into the phone.

Maybe not, thought Marvin.

Snow was coming down thick like God cut a pillow and all the feather down twirled to the ground in frosty clumps. Ankle deep, it cast a smooth layer of blinding white across the hardpan range from the cabin door to the distant black gash of the river.

Marvin blinked away freezing tears, knocked an icicle from his nose, and shuffled forward on boots wrapped in fuzzy coyote fur and twine string.

Along the river, marring the white horizon, Marvin counted ten vertical slash marks. Ten hackberry poles, each doing its part to hold the snow-covered telephone line high, like a chalk mark in the slate gray sky, an offering to heaven.

How proud.

To be able to talk across a distance, sight unseen.

To send dirty jokes and innuendo through a metal strand.

How proud, indeed.

Emil's cackle came again to Marvin's cold ears.

Wood axe in hand, he set out for the river.

That night, over a winning game table, Emil shared the dirt.

"Ida says you can get store-bought checkers at Belly's new mercantile in town."

He slurped the last of his puritan coffee and slid his game piece to the edge of the board.

"King me."

Marvin dropped a healthy dollop of rotgut into his own cup and stalled around scratching a pimple before topping his brother's rough-carved checker.

"If they're for sale at the mercantile, then it stands to reason they're store-bought," he said. "What's your point?"

Marvin only had four checkers left. The same number his brother had lost.

"I mean factory-made. Perfectly round and bright, painted red and black. Real nice sets, Ida says. Chess sets too, and decks of cards wrapped in paper."

"I ain't playing cards tonight," said Marvin. "And I'm tired of hearing about Ida."

With the telephone not working, she was still with them in spirit.

Omnipresent.

Emil sighed, picked his nose, then jumped two of Marvin's remaining men in a v-shaped move.

"Jump, jump. V-for-victory."

"Let's call it a night," said Marvin. "I got that animal husbandry book to read yet."

"Animal husbandry?"

"We got snow on the ground and calves on the way."

"I guess our gals don't need a husband. They all got the same one."

Marvin brushed the checkers into their wood box and drank from his cup.

"I mean Lucifer, the bull. I mean they

127

already got one husband."

Marvin carried the checkers to a shelf beside some jars of canned corn, then moved to his rocker beside the stove.

"That was a joke, Marvin. Animal husbandry."

"Yeah, yeah."

"I was just making a joke to pass the time. I guess I knew what you meant." Emil floundered at the table, tapped his fingers on the checkerboard. "Sure is lonesome without Ida. Without the telephone."

Marvin flipped open his hardback book, read the same page twice.

"What do you suppose could've happened?" said Emil.

"With what?"

"With the phone. What happened?"

"I wouldn't know."

"I sure hope Ida's okay."

"Why wouldn't she be? She's safe and sound in town."

"You think it's the weather? Maybe snow on the lines?"

Marvin thumbed the red blister on his palm with a wince. Even through his gloves, that axe rubbed his skin raw.

The pole came down harder than he'd thought it would.

"Wouldn't know."

"I do wonder what she's doing though."

"Probably driving her brother crazy."

"Oh, she ain't got no brother. She's an only child."

"I see."

"Lives in a little white house with green shutters. Flower garden out front. Right at the end of Taylor Street. You know where that is?"

"Albertson's only got one street. I guess I know it."

"You don't get to town much. I didn't think you knew the place."

"I don't recall it exactly, no. Just making a point about the town."

"When's the last time you went to town, Marvin?"

He thought back, counting the winters, counting the calving seasons.

"Five, six years, I suppose." Marvin closed the book on his finger, holding his place. "But that was just to haul some boys out of the pokey." He had a warm feeling beyond the heat of the stove. "I can remember a time before there was a town even there."

"One day you'll get civilized," said Emil. "You'll meet somebody just like I met Ida."

"I hope not."

"I sure hope she's okay."

As if in answer, the wood box on the wall

rang with a tremble that shook the cabin wall.

One short, two long. The line shack's ring.

"Heavens to Betsy!" said Emil, stumbling over his feet as he stretched to pull down the receiver. "Ida, honey? I was so worried. Yes. Yes. Yes."

Marvin pricked up his ears and chewed his tongue.

He'd worked himself to a lather that morning, taking the post down, cutting a wide hunk out of the line, burying the wire in the riverbank.

How could it be fixed already?

"Oh, my. Thank goodness. Oh, yes. Thank them for me too."

Marvin cranked his head around, looked over his shoulder at his brother with the question.

Emil covered the mouthpiece.

"Ida says the phone went out this morning. Lucky for us, her cousin is one of the men helped install the thing. Says those wormy hackberry poles tend to blow over easy in the wind. So him and some men rode out this afternoon and fixed it. Ain't that lucky?"

"Yeah. That's lucky."

"Ida says she wouldn't know what to do without the phone."

"I'll bet."

"No, no, sweetie. I was just talking to Mar-viiiiinnnn." He cackled, and Marvin pressed his blister hard enough to bring tears to his eyes.

Cutting the line wasn't the answer.

He'd have to get directly at the root.

Then and there, he made plans for a trip to town.

Later that week, the little white house with the green shutters at the end of Taylor street was quiet. At the nearest hitching rail, Marvin Dell climbed down from his horse, straightened his string tie, and fluffed up the flower bouquet he carried in a white-knuckled grip.

He walked toward the house.

The flowers were wild, a rough collection of late violet thistles and wilting sunflowers with a couple sprigs of cattail. Nothing as vibrant as the autumn rainbow of mums spackled with splotches of melting snow that decorated the front yard.

Marvin walked up the rock sidewalk, his pounding heart keeping time with boot steps that sounded unnaturally loud.

He rapped the door with bare knuckles and reached for his hat.

A beautiful blonde girl half his age opened

the door.

"Yes?" she said.

"Miss Tully?"

"Yes. Who are you?"

"Well, I'm . . . that is . . ." Caught like a drowning man in the violet-blue whirlpool of Ida's eyes, Marvin couldn't breathe.

He thrust forward the bouquet. "These are for you."

Blinking rapidly, Ida caught the flowers with both hands. "Thank you," she said. "I'm much obliged, I'm sure. But you still haven't told me your name."

Ida cupped the flowers to a swelling breast covered in clean blue gingham and planted a lightly closed fist on the swell of her hip. She wore loose-fitting trousers like a boy, but stood so the curves proved her a girl. She smelled of cucumbers and sandlewood.

Despite the cool breeze coming into town off the range, Marvin broke out in a sweat.

"I'm Marvin. Marvin Dell."

"Marvin?"

"I'm Emil Dell's brother."

Ida's smile outshone the garden of mums.

"Why didn't you say so? Dear, you must come in. Come in!"

Marvin let Ida lead him into a corner sitting room. The room was papered in a green floral swirl, furnished only with a squatting turquoise daybed and a small walnut secretary with a primitive three-legged stool. The rest of the house hid behind two closed white doors.

"Please sit down. Can I get you some tea?"

"I ought not to get too comfortable," said Marvin, trying to convince himself more than Ida. "I got something I need to tell you."

"Now that's a coincidence," Ida cocked her head and offered a mysterious smile. "But I'm sure whatever it is will go better over tea."

"Coincidence?"

"Make yourself at home," said Ida, passing through one of the white doors and leaving it open behind her. "I'll be right back."

Marvin sat down on the too-low daybed, palms cupping his knees. He heard Ida puttering around, moving pots and pans, humming to herself a happy, familiar tune. He imagined her flitting around in her gingham blouse and pants that showed off every curve, casting her bright smile and deep blue eyes at cups of black tea topped off with cream, sweetened with sugar.

He pictured her soft voice, her hair, her skin. Thought of her making tea. Making dinner.

Stitching a woolen sock.

He pictured that smile turning fast when he told her what he had to say.

He stood up abruptly. Almost fled.

And then, through the open door, he saw the telephone.

Screwed to the wall, its mouthpiece and looped receiver drooping down, it was a brooding vulture waiting for dark. A wooden box with a dark purpose, waiting to claim the souls of his brother and the innocent young beauty humming her way back to him.

Marvin wouldn't let the monster win.

He was going to go through with his plan.

Ida came through the door holding a silver tray with steaming cups and saucers, restoring Marvin's resolve.

"I've got something to tell you," he said. "Before I lose my nerve."

Ida's face was open with curiosity. "Go ahead," she said.

Fight fire with fire.

But how to fight a monster?

With another monster.

A green-eyed monster.

"Emil is fixing to get married."

To her credit, Ida didn't so much as flinch at the news.

Instead, she set the tray on the flat writing

surface of the secretary, then handed him a cup.

"Do sit down," she said.

Marvin sat.

"Did you hear what I said?"

"About Emil getting married?"

"Yes."

"Yes," she sipped her tea. "I suppose I knew it might happen."

"You did?"

"Yes, of course," she said, "In fact, it's what I meant when I said it was a coincidence that you had something to tell me. Because I have something to tell you."

Now it was Marvin's turn to be curious.

"These nightly calls with Emil on the telephone," said Ida. "I haven't been in favor of them. I want you to know that."

"You haven't?"

"No," said Ida. "I have not. And the news you've just given me only confirms my opinion of that damnable box."

"Your opinion?" Marvin couldn't believe his ears.

Ida's face was a storm of emotion. "Frankly speaking, I hate the thing." She set her tea down on her lap and raised both hands to the sky. "I know all the arguments. It's a blessing in an emergency. It brings the community closer together." Her blue eyes

135

flashed with the tempest of her anger. "Well I think it tears people apart. It makes intimate moments like this one — between you and me — irrelevant."

Marvin felt himself blushing.

"It's come between friends and family. It's come between men and women. Excuse me for saying it, but that rotten brother of yours has nearly ruined my life."

"I had no idea," said Marvin. "No idea."

His plan to break up Emil and Ida now seemed pointless.

Ida's features softened and, breathless, she batted her eyelashes. "I must apologize. I do get carried away."

His big idea to plant the made-up story of another woman in Ida's mind, to relate an imaginary betrayal wasn't necessary.

Ida herself was ending the affair.

Or was she?

Marvin sipped his tea.

Something didn't add up.

He looked around the room, saw the stain where the ceiling leaked, noted the old bottle of ink, the yellowing envelopes on the secretary.

"How long have you lived here?" he said.

"All my life."

"And how long is that?"

"I'll be 23 next month."

"And you live alone?"

Ida put her hand to her throat. "Alone? I don't understand."

"Alone," said Marvin. "As in, nobody else in the house."

"Nobody but mother of course." Her lips curved and she laughed. "But you're teasing me now, Mr. Dell. You know that darned good and well. After all, weren't we just talking about her and your brother?"

"Your mother?"

"Yes?"

"Your mother talks on the phone with Emil?"

"Naturally?"

Marvin swallowed the rest of his tea with a hasty gulp. Again, he stood.

"I'm the one that needs to apologize, Ida. I think there's been a mistake."

The girl stood too.

"Ida? That's mom's name." She narrowed her eyes and peered at him with a grin. "You didn't think . . . ?"

Marvin nodded.

"I'm afraid I did."

"My name is Velda. I'm Ida's daughter. I've never talked to your brother in my life."

Marvin blinked twice.

"But I have to say, it's a pleasure to finally meet you."

Velda's firm hand on his arm pushed him back to the daybed.

"From everything that mom says, you and me think a lot alike." Velda took his cup. "Would you like some more tea?" she said.

"I wouldn't say no," he said.

"Shall we talk about the telephone some more?"

"I'd prefer something more . . . intimate," said the no-longer confirmed bachelor.

"With nothing between us," said Velda.

"Forget the tea," said Marvin, and he reached for her hand.

Killing Hilda Kempker

Barney Bogart, dressed like a cowboy with long sleeves, vest, and chaparrals, and riding an old roan, didn't think of himself as a bad fellar — which is probably where he and Stank Carmichael differed.

Stank, riding at Barney's side on a gray gelding and dressed like a citified dandy (complete with brown English bowler), saw the two of them as rough and tumble outlaws. "Real owlhoots on the dark ways prod," he'd sometimes say. "Jail broke desperadoes."

The two hadn't so much broke jail as simply walked out of a Colorado cell during the guard's drunken lunch hour.

Be that as it may, they were now headed for Stank's hometown of Emoryville on the green flint hills of Kansas.

It was Sunday, and mischief was in the air.

"I want it to look like an accident, dammit," said Stank, throwing back a slug from the brown bottle of corn mash he'd taken off a passing medicine wagon the day before.

"You're putting quite a hurt on that bottle. Why not share a drink?" said Barney.

Stank belched, loud and proud, and shoved the cork back into the long neck. "It's not the bottle I'm fixin' to hurt. It's Hilda Kempker."

Sometimes Barney and Stank were the best of friends, sometimes all they could manage was to grunt back and forth. Since Stank had started nursing his obsession with Hilda Kempker, Barney wasn't sure he knew his saddle pard at all.

"You think about her way too much," said Barney.

"Promised myself I'd take care of her —"

"More than twelve years ago, I know," said Barney, finishing the sentence. He'd heard it often enough during their journey across Kansas.

"Round-up season's starting soon," Barney said. "Maybe we ought to look for a job."

A ragged, black buzzard swooped low over Stank's bowler toward the line of buildings that began to emerge on the horizon.

"Hilda Kempker's the only job on my mind, buddy. She's right up there in Emoryville. Probably still sitting in that same stinkin' oak chair in the church basement."

Hilda had been Stank's Sunday School teacher.

Among other things.

"Wasn't she married to your old man for a while?" said Barney.

"Nah," Stank lied. "You're thinking of somebody else."

But Barney knew he wasn't.

"We need two things to do this right," said Stank.

"I don't think there's much right about knocking off your Sunday School teacher." Barney's horse nickered again, as if in agreement. "Besides, you and me are wanted men."

Stank ignored the commentary of man and beast alike, continuing to stitch together the threadbare tapestry of his plan.

"See there's this Indian story, from the Poncas, I think, about how they make poison arrows. You got any idea how Poncas make poison arrows?"

Barney thought Stank was getting his tribes confused, but the breeze across the hills continued to smell sweet like blooming alfalfa, and the sun was bright but not overly hot.

He felt like he had plenty of time to listen.

141

"I ain't never seen a poison arrow. And I hope I never do. Especially not sticking out of me."

Stank took another drink from his bottle and explained himself.

"Here's how they do it. How we're gonna do it too. First, you get yourself a rattle-snake."

"Seems easy enough."

"Then you procure yourself a good piece of liver. You make the snake bite the liver a bunch of times."

"Over and over," said Barney.

"Over and over, that's right," said Stank. "You saturate the liver with poison. Then you dry it."

"Takes a while to dry," said Barney.

"Then you grind it into a powder and coat the tips of your arrows with the poison."

"And that really works?"

Stank nodded. "Foolproof," he said.

"So you're planning to shoot ol' Hilda with an arrow? Don't seem like anybody'd see that as much of an accident. Didn't you want it to look like an accident?"

"I was just explaining the organ of my idea."

"You mean the origin of your idea."

"We're gonna feed her rattlesnake poison in her tea." The more he spoke, the more

142

animated he got. For a minute, Barney was afraid Stank would fall off and be trampled by his gelding.

"See, instead of liver, you get a big ol' sack of tea."

"And you have the rattlesnake whale into it," said Barney.

"Right."

"And then you give it Hilda. Maybe sort of as a remembrance gift. Like maybe you play-act like you're happy to see her."

"Right."

"And then," said Barney, getting into the spirit of things, "she goes home, pours some tea into her cup, adds a little water, takes a sip, and bam!" He slapped his hands together. "She falls over dead. Just like that."

Stank agreed. "Just like that."

"Won't work," said Barney.

Stank reined his horse into a tight circle. "What'cha mean it won't work?"

"It won't work, that's all. A body don't die if you drink rattlesnake venom. Especially if it's all diluted down by hot water and tea and such."

"I don't believe it."

"It's true," said Barney, making things up on the fly. "I talked to a doctor once who said so. He said your guts just digest the stuff and it passes on through."

143

Stank shook his head, looking off into the distance.

But Barney knew Stank believed him.

Now Emoryville was a solid string of buildings on either side of the trail, interspersed with clumps of young trees. On the far edge of town, the spire of the Methodist church steeple soared into a hard, blue sky.

If Barney didn't say something soon, Stank was liable to mope right up to the steps of the church and gun down the old bag in cold blood.

And then where would they be?

In the soup, that's where.

He didn't actually mind killing Hilda Kempker. He didn't care one way or the other. He just didn't want to be around when it happened.

Barney searched his mind for something to suggest. "Here's an idea for you," he said finally. "You ever heard of Scheele's Green?"

Stank kept his gaze on the trail and just barely shook his head.

"Well it's a kind of stuff they use to make wallpaper and other green things. Only it ain't healthy like all this green around us. In fact, it's got so much arsenic in it that — let's say you licked some wallpaper — it'd kill you instantly."

Barney closed his eyes and crossed his

hands over his chest for effect. His partner cranked his head around, obviously taken with the idea.

"You ain't kidding?"

"I ain't kidding. I heard some egghead say they think it might've been what killed Napoleon."

And that part was true. He wasn't making it up!

Stank leaned back in the saddle, tipping his bowler cap forward. "Say," he said. "This might have possibilities."

"Like what are you thinkin'?"

"Find some wallpaper, soak it in the tea?"

"Maybe," said Barney nodding. "Maybe. How about we just scrape some of that green off into a powder and put it in a pepper shaker?"

Stank stroked his chin. "I like it. I like it. Except . . ."

"Except what?"

"Except as long as I knew her, Hilda Kempker didn't take pepper. Or salt. Or spices of any kind on her food."

"We sneak in and slip it into her dinner," Barney suggested.

"She cooks everything herself. She doesn't eat at restaurants." Stank's voice was dropping along with his enthusiasm. "And on top of that, where we gonna find this green wallpaper? I mean, how would we know we had this steel green stuff in the first place?"

Now it was Barney's turn to mope.

"I s'pect you're right," he said.

Emoryville enjoyed a peaceful Sunday afternoon as the pair rode onto the main street. They passed a couple squatty, gray, frame houses, one without much foundation, that sunk a little to the left. An impressive, two-story brick building held down the first block with a cornerstone reading 1890. On the next corner ahead, the Methodist church.

With nobody on the street, Barney and Stank took the time to lollygag. Barney shook his head at the big building.

"Mighty high airs, puttin' up a brick monstrosity like that. Looks like your little hometown done grown past its raising."

"They always was a snooty bunch," said Stank. "Why do you think I left?"

Across the street and down a yellow pine wood boardwalk, another new building waited, this one with a false front and a string of shining tin signs. A row of barrels rested in the shadow of a blue-striped canvas awning, its corners gently moving in the breeze.

"Looks like the town's growing left and right."

A smiling boy on a bicycle rounded the corner by the Methodist Church. Barney nodded in response to his friendly wave.

"We still ain't figured what to do with Hilda," said Barney. "Might be best to forget that part of our visit?"

"Forget?" said Stank. "No, sir. I'll never forget. She's a mean woman, I tell you. You ask anybody. Everybody knows her. And everybody hates her. Why, it'd be nothing less than divine justice if that there church steeple tipped over and skewered her right through the heart."

From under his hat, Barney glanced up at the narrow spire, blinding white in the afternoon sun. Looked solid enough for now . . . .

"There's a window there in the lower part," said Stank. "Rather than the steeple itself, what if something fell out of that window and landed on her?"

Barney closed one eye and followed Stank's outstretched finger.

"Something like what?"

"Cannon ball?" said Stank.

"You got one handy?"

"All right," said Stank, hands on his hips. "What if one of the bells tumbled out?"

Then he snapped his fingers. "Look at that wood siding up there. Why, if one of them

147

boards came loose and got caught in the wind . . ."

"I don't know," said Barney, picturing the accident in his mind.

"We were trying to be too clever is all," said Stank. "This way it's cut and dried."

"Gettin' Hilda into position, that's gonna be the hard part."

"Naw. Here, lemme show you."

The church was a long, rectangular frame structure stretching from the street back toward an open hay field with expertly trimmed glass on either side. The front doors faced the street with the steeple directly overhead. Stank climbed down from the roan and walked to a spot in front of the doors, directly underneath the high steeple, its long shadow pointing like a finger to the northeast.

"What if we met her coming out of church, and stopped her right here?"

Barney crawled off his roan and kept his eye on the steeple, walking backwards into the street. He looked at Stank.

Then the steeple.

Then Stank.

"Back about two feet," said Barney.

Stank stepped back. "Here?"

"More or less. Maybe put a mark on the ground."

Stank nodded, fished for the folding knife he kept in his pocket.

Then there was the creak of metal hinges and a voice from the door of the church.

"Help you boys?"

Barney raised his eyebrows, then extended a hand to the old gent that lurched down the wood steps toward them.

"Howdy do," he said. "We're just, uh . . . admiring your church here."

"It's a beaut," the man agreed. "Didn't catch your names?"

"I'm John Smith," said Barney, using the names they'd used at the Colorado jail. "This here is my brother Joe. Who am I talking to?"

"I'm Sam Norris." He stroked the uneven patch of whiskers on his chin, paying special attention to Stank. "Joe Smith, eh? You got a mighty familiar look about you."

"Never been here before," said Stank, toeing the dirt.

"But that don't mean we ain't heard about Emoryville," said Barney. "In fact, we heard you got a right fine Methodist congregation here. Folks talk about it all along the cow trails."

"Is that so?" said Sam.

"It is indeed. In fact," Barney shot Stank a wink, "we heard tell you got an especially good Sunday School."

Sam scratched his head and peered at Barney through half-closed eyes.

"Ain't had much Sunday School for a while."

"Oh? How come?" said Barney.

"Sad tale to tell you," said Sam. "It breaks my heart to say it."

For the first time since Sam appeared, Stank raised his head and walked straight up to the man.

He looked a little too eager to hear the story.

Or scared.

With worry in his voice, he said, "What happened?"

"Our beloved teacher, Hilda Kempker, passed tragically."

"Hilda? Gone? How?" Stank's voice cracked a little.

"Happened right here on the lawn in the shadow of the steeple. Just a few feet from where we're standing," said Sam.

"Shadow of the steeple? Then what?"

Sam nodded, obviously enjoying the anticipation on Stank's face.

"Church picnic."

"Hard to imagine anything bad happening at a picnic," said Barney

"Just an accident," said Sam with a shrug.

Or rather, a series of them.

"How's that?"

"Well old Hilda stood up and took a drink from her cup. She must've swallowed her tea the wrong way —"

"Tea?"

"Green tea," said Sam.

"G-green?"

"Yup. Anyway, she sorta staggered back, and as luck would have it, one of the siding boards up there on the steeple picked just that minute to fall."

"And it hit her on the head?"

"Yes, it did, but that ain't what killed her."

"Oh my goodness."

"After that board hits her, Hilda takes a few more steps and falls down beside the steps back there."

"And a rattlesnake bites her," said Barney.

"Well, no," said Sam. "But that's not a bad guess."

"An . . . an arrow maybe?" said Stank. "Did somebody shoot her with an arrow?"

"Arrow?" said Sam with a chuckle. "You boys are full of the devil. Where would an arrow come from? In case you ain't heard, this ain't the wild west anymore."

"So what killed her?"

Sam pointed at his throat.

"Piece of raw liver."

"Raw liver?"

"A favorite indulgence of some of the old folks around here. Caught right here in her windpipe when that board hit." Sam shook his head. "I tell you, when He puts his mind to it, the good Lord has some creative ways to dispatch a body."

"He . . . he sure does," said Stank.

Barney took off his hat.

The three stood there for a minute, only the sound of Stank's stuffed-up nose breaking the silence.

"I guess we ought to be riding on," Barney said finally.

Stank nodded, shook Sam's hand in farewell, and followed his partner to the horses.

Side by side, they rode out of Emoryville, Stank blowing his nose and dabbing at his leaky eyes.

"Sorta makes you think, doesn't it?" said Stank.

"It does at that," said Barney. It made him think that with old Hilda gone they might finally talk about something else.

"I mean, it's an awful coincidence, ain't it, Barney?"

Barney chewed on it a while, then spit it out. "That damned galoot was stretching things. I bet he made half of it up as he was standing there."

Stank shook his head, reined his gelding to a full stop. As the dust settled around them, Barney could see tears still streaming down Stank's face.

"I don't think so. I think it was all true. But I don't think it's a coincidence."

"The hell you say."

Stank's shoulders drooped with defeat. "Don't you see, Barney? After all them lessons I ignored, after all these years of struggle, that darned Hilda Kempker's reached out from the grave to convert me."

"Now, Stank, don't you think maybe you're —"

Stank held his head high. "I'm sorry. That's the way I see it, Barney." He turned his face back toward town. "I've seen the light."

Barney wasn't sure what to say, so he stayed quiet as Stank gently steered his horse back toward the direction they'd come from. "I think I'm going back. To stay."

"To stay? What about round-up season? What about finding a job? Doggone-it, Stank! What're you gonna do?"

Stank looked over his shoulder and for the first time that Barney could remember, Stank's cheeks were creased with a genuine smile.

"I hear they got an opening for a Sunday School teacher," he said.

AKA: The DaVinci Kid

The new Opera House in Randolph City, Wyoming, didn't hold as many patrons as some of the theater buildings cropping up on the plains during this industrious spring of 1898, but on its opening night, it was far and away the busiest place Riley Boone and I had ever visited together. That intimidating fact, plus Riley's natural interest in science and engineering, might have been why he ignored the people and the play and focused instead on the building's interior and the glowing apparatus he called a Drummond Lamp. From the corner of my eye, I watched as he took in the tiered balcony extending above and behind our third-row chairs. Then his gaze whirled around to the curtained box seats hanging over the hard wood stage. Then he was back to the lamp.

"Brilliance made possible by an oxyetheric torch, if I'm not mistaken," said Riley. "If you notice the peculiar juxtaposition of the horizontal liquid ether tank with the more traditional oxygen hose, you'll see something really unique. And more than a tad bit dangerous. In fact, it was this very style of lamp that was behind the great debacle in Paris earlier this year. I'm sure you read about it?"

This being the climax of *My Schenectady Gal's* first act, the portly theater patron on my right wasn't especially happy with Riley's nattering on and let me know with a high-browed glare. As the town marshal's daughter, I wasn't exactly a society queen, and with my carrot top and freckles, I certainly didn't pretend to be one. Still, I wore my best dress, and nobody was going to question Lacey Dale's manners again. I poked my elbow into Riley's heavy black top coat.

"Lacey, if you please," he said, pushing up his round spectacles. "I'm surprised at you. I mean, I can understand your wanting to postpone more conversation, but to resort to such rude behavior as —" I elbowed him again but motioned with my eyes toward Portly. "Ah. Well, this is awkward, indeed," said Riley. Then, leaning directly across my lap, he did his best impersonation of a normal person. "I'm sorry," he said, an apol-

156

ogy that earned him another scornful look.

Naturally, after three months stepping out with Riley, I was fairly used to scornful looks. My awkward, watchmaker boyfriend simply didn't understand people at all, and it was something I was doing my best to change. The main problem was Riley didn't regularly set foot outside his workshop, a building occupied twenty years before by none other than Thomas Alva Edison when he passed through Wyoming on (of all things) an expedition to view the 1878 solar eclipse.

Not only had I taken it upon myself to see that Riley got out more, I hoped to introduce him to *real culture.* Noticing how long his wild, blonde curls were getting, I decided I'd have to introduce him to a sharp pair of scissors quite soon, as well. Still and all, his dress was fine for the occasion, if not exactly colorful, with a white cotton shirt and black leather shoes, braces, and trousers.

"Just hush up and watch the play," I told Riley, but I could see he was again entranced with the lamp.

"I'm afraid I'm just not much for these affairs of the heart," he whispered. "I'd much rather get down there and inspect that lamp. Doesn't it bother you, Lacey? It certainly bothers me." I nudged him a third time and he clammed up.

Smoke from nearby cigars swirled within the brilliant beams of light aimed center stage at John Rudolph, amateur actor, professional carpenter. He had stringy brown hair and a ragged mustache that looked like it was trimmed every few weeks with a dull pocket knife. His suit coat and pants were equally rumpled, and that wasn't part of his stage persona. Actually, for Mr. Rudolph, rumpled was a compliment. By way of contrast, the stage set was a tidy affair: a wooden folding chair, a table with a glass of water, and a red upholstered daybed. Behind it all was a tall canvas with an apartment interior painted on it.

The whole town was packed into the new venue tonight, or at least anybody who was anybody was here. From where we sat in the third row, I saw the mayor, several local merchants, Doc Hamilton and his daughter, Ilsa, and my own father, John Dale, the town marshal. As usual, Dad hadn't bothered to remove his tall Stetson hat, and he wore his usual jeans, work shirt, and fringed leather vest. We sat on fine, wooden folding chairs like the one on the stage, the first half-dozen rows padded with thick cushions, embroidered and put into place by the ladies of the First Congregational Church.

The piano man at stage left started a song that signaled a change of scenes, and I turned back to the stage.

Standing tall, Rudolph lifted the water glass to his lips, swallowed, set the glass down, and promptly dropped to the stage floor with a thud. It took the audience a minute or two to realize the tumble had nothing to do with Rudolph's acting ability and so, at first, and with the music continuing, they offered enthusiastic applause.

Under the expert direction of the Grim Reaper, Oscar Rudolph nearly got a standing ovation.

"Lacey," said Riley, "did you just notice something odd?"

"You mean other than Mr. Rudolph's hitting the floor?"

"Yes, that's absolutely what I mean," said Riley. "The lamp —"

"Oh, forget about the lamp," I said.

"He's dead," whispered Mr. Portly, then more loudly, "By Jupiter, I believe Rudolph is dead!"

"Yes, indeed," said Riley. "It's what I'm afraid of. I just happened to notice that —"

A lady in front of us screamed.

"Honestly, I didn't notice anything," I said.

Another cry launched a short symphony

159

of copycat bleats and moans, and then the audience was on the move. Women shuffled in orbit around their chairs, reaching out to one another with whispered chatter. A few men leapt into the aisle like they meant business, then shoved their hands into their pockets when they realized there was no business to be had. Nobody approached the stage, and the rumpled Rudolph stayed stretched out flat, with his still-open eyes staring out at the crowd.

Riley lifted his head to peer above the people in front of us. "If I could just get another clear look," he said. "Pardon me, ma'am," he said, swiveling around the chair before him and stepping up to the seat.

Before he could step past the swooning girl, I grabbed his coattail and yanked him back. "Get down from there."

"Here's the marshal now," said someone behind me.

Sure enough, Dad was in the center aisle, making his way to the front of the room. When he reached the short series of steps leading to the stage, he stopped, turned, and started waving his arms.

"Quiet down now, everybody. Quiet down." Slowly but surely, he gained the attention of the crowd. "Doc Hamilton is here," he said, as the doc made his way

160

through the audience, hurrying toward the steps and stage right. While Doc examined the body, Dad scratched at his thick salt and pepper mustache and said, "Mr. Rudolph appears to have suffered some sort of, uh . . . ailment?" He looked over his shoulder to see the doctor shaking his head.

Riley's attention was fixed on the stage. "I absolutely need to speak with the doctor," he said. "Urgently, I'm afraid. Why, this is horrible." He pushed against me, but I held him back. "I must see the doctor," he said.

"Oh, Riley, you're not ill?"

He cocked his head with that puzzled look he reserved for old women and children. And young girls. And teenage boys. And most small animals. "Of course, I'm not ill. Why would you think I was ill?"

"For the time being, I'm going to ask everybody to stay where you are while we get this sorted out," said Dad, cupping his hands around his mouth so he could be heard over the noise from the crowd.

The crowd booed and groaned, and the marshal held up his hands.

"I know. I know. But I'm going to have to ask you to be patient for a few minutes."

Riley put his hand on my arm. "Wait here," he said, and squeezed past me.

"I will not." Excusing myself, I pushed

past Mr. Portly and followed Riley into the aisle. Once there, we started toward the front, but not before I noticed Doc Hamilton's daughter, Ilsa, in her place in the row across from us. While everyone else was working to get a better view, or chattering with their neighbors, Ilsa remained seated and aloof, dressed in her finest, stroking the black hair at her shoulder as if the long bundle were a cat.

Among smells of bay rum cologne and lye soap, I moved through the crowd, the noise of conversation loud in my ears as I joined Riley and Dad at the foot of the stage.

"Marshal Dale. Excuse me, sir? I'd like to have a word with the doctor, if I might," said Riley.

"Oh, good! Here's the watchmaker. Only a matter of time 'til you showed up." Dad gave me a dirty look. "Lacey, tell your friend to mind his own business."

Since taking up residence in town, Riley had inserted himself into more than one of Dad's criminal investigations.

"He doesn't mean any harm," I said. In fact, Riley had solved more than one case with his knowledge of science and modern invention.

"Indeed, I don't. And when I speak with the doctor, I think you'll find that I'm a great deal of help."

"Why?" said Dad.

"There's no doubt in my mind the doctor will find the contents of that water glass most interesting," Riley said, ignoring the steps and climbing easily to the stage, sidestepping the Drummond lamp to approach the table and water glass. I followed quickly behind.

During the theater's construction, Riley had explained to me how the limelights worked (more or less), how a ball of quicklime was suspended in front of a blowtorch inside a mirrored canister. White hot, the lime produced dazzling light that was directed at the stage. This particular lamp was a conglomeration of parts mounted on a wheeled iron framework. There was a horizontal cylindrical tank attached to the light canister with rubber hoses. Presumably, gas in the tank fed the burning torch. Standing in the spotlight, Riley crouched down to peer into the glass of water, and that's when I noticed it gave off an eerie blue glow.

Is that what Riley had noticed?

Did he suspect Rudolph had been poisoned?

I reached for the glass, but Riley stopped me with a warning.

"Don't drink it," he said.

163

Riley picked up the glass and walked closer to the light, tipping it back and forth in the intense white beam. As he moved, the glow intensified. "I think I have something here," he said.

"What in thunder's going on? Put that water away and get down from there," said Dad.

"What is it, son?" said Doc Hamilton, standing beside the corpse, casually dusting his hands.

Riley began to reply, but was interrupted by a voice from stage left.

"Coming through," said a thin-whiskered stage hand named Gil Wilkens. Dressed in butternut pants, cotton shirt, and tan braces, he quickly stomped past Riley to clutch the handles of the Drummond light and swing it around. "Watch out, now," said Wilkens, leaning back to pull the heavy cart with its tank and hoses and blazing canister. I watched him wheel the big cart away from Riley into place three feet to the right of Doc Hamilton. The canvas flat was awash in illumination and a hundred shadows popped up all around them.

"There you go, Doc. Thought that might help you see better?"

Wilkens fiddled with one of the nozzles that fed the torch.

The light wasn't shining on the crime scene at all.

"Why, yes, I suppose," said the puzzled Hamilton. "Thank you, Mr. Wilkens."

Again, Wilkens seemed to be adjusting something. Then he stepped back and, with an odd expression on his face, a mixture of triumph and anticipation, tipped his hat.

"Look out!" said Riley, and I pushed Dad down to the base of the stage.

Riley came down beside us as a vermillion ball of fire blossomed across the stage like some immense garden flower. The charred air immediately filled with the stink of hot ether, and for one crazy second, a thought raced through my mind.

The opening night's performance had brought down the house!

On stage, the thunderous force of the Drummond lamp's explosion sent metal shards flying into the ceiling, across the stage, and into the audience. As the crowd surged for the door with a variety of cries and caterwauls, I said a silent prayer that nobody would be trampled.

"Good night, nurse!" said Dad.

For a handful of moments, crouched down at the foot of the stage, with nothing but chaos around us, Riley kept his hand on my shoulder. When I looked at him, his smile was sincere, and it would've brought tears to my eyes had I not immediately been distracted by a crack in the lens of his glasses. "Riley, you've ruined your spectacles," I said.

"Hmm?" He pulled his head backwards and looked down his nose. "So I have." Then: "How's the marshal?"

"Are you all right, Dad?" I said.

"Well enough," he said, patting himself as he stood. "And you?"

I assured him that Riley and I were no worse for wear, and he called to some men nearby. "Make sure nothing's caught fire."

"Anybody hurt up there?" said one of the men.

"We're okay."

The same couldn't be said for Doc Hamilton. The poor fellow had taken the brunt of the blast and lay on top of Rudolph's corpse, an equally lifeless heap.

Bodies were literally beginning to stack up.

"Nelson! Gunderson!" Dad shouted at two of his deputies. "See how badly folks are hurt." Miraculously, as we would discover during the next few days, none of the theater patrons were seriously injured. With an odd assortment of small cuts and light bruises from the contained blast, it seemed they did more harm to each other trying to escape the auditorium. "Get that bunch under control," said Dad, marching away.

"Another deliberate attempt, I think," said Riley.

I brushed at Riley's dark coat. "You think Wilkens tampered with the light?"

"I do," said Riley. "There can be little doubt. Once he realized what I'd ascertained about the water, he deliberately moved the light. Did you notice? He pretended to be helping the doctor, but the light didn't shine on the crime scene at all."

"But you're okay? You're not hurt?" I pulled a stray bit of rubbish from his hair.

"Why, no, Lacey. Are you?"

"No, I . . ."

Gently, I pushed the cracked spectacles up his nose.

"I just don't know how I would . . . . If you were hurt, I mean . . ." I let my words trail off when I realized Riley wasn't listening.

I followed his eyes, turned to see Ilsa Hamilton, the doctor's daughter rushing toward us. I reached out, but she brushed past, sobbing, a look of twisted anguish on her face. Despite her long dress, she took the short set of steps in two strides and stood on the ruined stage amidst a scattering of charred brass and twisted iron.

"To lose her father in such a gruesome manner," I said.

But Ilsa didn't so much as glance at Hamilton's remains. Instead, she ran to and fro around the radius of the blast, under the box seats, behind curtains, and back to the front of the stage.

"It doesn't appear to be her father she's worried about," said Riley.

Ilsa spun from side to side, bouncing impatiently, pulling at her long, black hair.

"Can we help you, Miss?" said Riley. He climbed to the stage, but stopped as Ilsa frantically looked to the left, to the right. "Where's Gil?" she said through her tears. "Where's Gil?"

"Gil is Mr. Wilkens' first name," I reminded Riley.

"Where is he?" she cried, and stepped back again. Now she was directly under one of the curtained box seats, its railing and banners dark with soot from the explosion. "Where's Gil?"

Riley held both hands forward in a reassuring manner. "Mr. Wilkens isn't here," he said.

I realized he was right.

Rudolph and the doc were still where they fell. If he'd been caught in the blast, Wilkens should have been there too. But he wasn't.

"There's Wilkens now," said Riley from the stage. Across the auditorium, weaving his way in and out among the last of the crowd, I saw him. Butternut pants, cotton shirt and braces. The marshal was only two steps away.

"Dad! Stop that man. Butternut pants!"

Just as I saw Dad reach for Wilkens, Ilsa issued a demand.

"No, you don't," she said.

On stage, Riley was a statue. Ilsa had a small two-barrel Remington Derringer pointed at his chest. "Back away," she told him.

"Please, Miss," said Riley. "If you'd take a moment to observe the situation, I'm sure you would see that it's quite precarious. In fact, I would advise you to take at least three or four steps forward. Well, six might be best."

"I don't think so," said Ilsa.

"It's not for my sake, you understand," Riley explained. "I'm merely trying to be of some service. Frankly, I don't think you're paying attention to what's going on around you."

I told you my boyfriend doesn't understand people. Especially wild-eyed lunatics.

"You did it together, didn't you?" I said to Ilsa. "You and Wilkens killed Rudolph. Then your father."

She smiled casually.

"What do you know about it, Cowgirl?" she said.

"Please," said Riley. "I really must insist we discuss this elsewhere."

"Insist?" said Ilsa. "The cowgirl's boyfriend insists. What are you, some kind of gunslinger? I don't see any pistols on you, mister."

I climbed to the stage. "He's a scientist," I said. "And Riley," I said, "I do think we should discuss it now."

I directed a question to him. "Was Mr. Rudolph poisoned?"

"Well, yes, Lacey, I believe so, but we need —"

"Shush," I said. "How do you know it?"

"Esculin," he said. "I noticed it almost immediately after Rudolph collapsed."

"Noticed what?"

"You'll recall I saw something odd. You see, just like esculin in solution, the water in the glass was giving off a faint blue florescence under the intense light of the Drummond lamp. The effect was described by Dr. Eugene Lommel in the February 1876 issue of the *Popular Science* monthly.

170

It's my hypothesis the water was tainted with the intent of harming Mr. Rudolph."

"Nope, not a gunslinger," said Ilsa.

"Or maybe the intent was to harm Dr. Hamilton," I said. "To set up an incident that would bring him to the stage where he could be killed in an accident. With the entire town as witness, nobody would ever question it."

"Naturally, Ilsa would have easy access to her father's store of chemicals," said Riley "But why would a beautiful young woman want to kill her father?"

Beautiful?!

"Thank you for that," said Ilsa.

"Riley, you're not much for affairs of the heart," I said. "Or for paying attention to what's going on in town. Rumors have been flying about Ilsa and Gil Wilkens for weeks. About how Ilsa's father disapproved of their relationship."

"You talk too much," said Ilsa, jabbing the pistol toward me.

"Drop the gun." Dad's voice came from the main floor. Beside him, was Wilkens, his head hanging low, his wrists clamped together in irons.

"I won't," said Ilsa, closing one eye as if to aim. "You'll have to take me —"

As if on cue, Riley Boone covered the

distance between himself and Ilsa in one, enormous leap, slamming the girl to the hard wood floor beyond, sending the small pistol flying even as a heavy oak railing from the box seat above crashed into the spot where she'd stood only seconds before.

"I tried to warn you," said Riley as he climbed to his feet. "Perhaps now we can finish discussing the situation over here."

Outside, later that night, a fat bank of moonlit clouds rode the far horizon west away from Randolph City. Holding tight to Riley's arm, I stepped lightly down the dusty road toward the modest frame house Dad and I shared.

"He may not have shown it, but the marshal was proud of you tonight," I said.

"He's a fine lawman," said Riley.

"And you're a fine scientist," I said.

"It was Mr. Edison who left so much behind in my workshop. All those journals and equipment. Half-finished experiments. There's a lot to study."

"A pity about Ilsa Hamilton. Wilkens too." I made a clucking sound with my tongue. "Love leads people do odd things."

For once, Riley was quiet.

"The foolish chances a person takes," I said. "The opportunities one passes by." I watched a pair of cowboys lead their horses down the street. "The serious contemplation of love can drive you mad. And the silly bits make you laugh."

"Silly bits?"

"When Ilsa called you a gunslinger."

"You called me a scientist."

"My DaVinci Kid," I said.

"What?"

"It just sort of popped into my mind."

"I'm primarily a clockmaker."

"As such, perhaps you can think up a way to stop time."

Then I kissed him right there in the middle of the dusty street, and it felt as if time did indeed stop.

If only for that instant.

GRAND DESIGN

As one of the younger settlements on the Wyoming range, Randolph City's cemetery is small in acreage and big in sentiment. Spattered with wildflowers and smelling of cut grass, there's a wild beauty appropriate to the souls who rest there. The enormous gravestones are proportional — dad would say indirectly — to the character of those old-timers. Founders (all men) whose pioneer spirits outshined the sordid details of their life.

It seemed impossible to bury 18-year-old Elly Benteen there.

Several years older, I was Elly's senior — but I could think of no place worse for my own eternal rest.

To bed down amongst the town fathers gave me the willies, as I'm sure it would Elly.

If she weren't dead, I mean.

Marching along with a solemn procession

of mourners under a clear summer sky toward the graveyard's iron gates, I wondered what kind of marker Elly Benteen's father picked for her.

Big Sam, breeder of prize-winning stallions, was the second wealthiest man in the region, after Charles Murry. Sam Benteen could afford the best.

The summer wind pelted us with dust and next to me, Dad dabbed at his eyes.

"Be strong, Lacey," he said, and I gave his hand a squeeze. Marshal John Dale wasn't one to cry in public, but the loss of one so young and pretty to the fever had everyone in a tizzy.

Except, apparently, for my boyfriend Riley Boone, who fidgeted under one of only two trees for miles around, next to the cemetery fence, next to one of the diggers, toeing the dirt pile and cocking his head to the left and right, watching with open curiosity as Elly's four old uncles lugged their dreadful cargo to the edge of a two-foot riser.

They set the coffin down and I caught Riley's smiling eyes with a furrowed brow of my own.

Show some respect, why don't you?

He nodded a head of shaggy blonde hair, letting his wire-rimmed spectacles slide to the tip of his nose.

He silently mouthed something to me, surreptitiously pointing at the coffin.

I shrugged. "I don't understand," I whispered.

"Ours is not to understand the ways of the Lord," said dad, snuffing above his thick red mustache.

"I wasn't talking to you," I said.

At the gravesite, the line of three dozen dispersed, leaving the old folks and ladies to perch on a succession of wooden folding chairs set in place earlier in the day by members of the First Congregational Church. The community leaders stood glumly at the side of the pit with the preacher. Big Sam commanded a position front and center, his round belly straining the buttons on a white silk shirt, his tall Stetson hat blocking the view of the ladies seated behind.

He stared at the hole in the ground with puffy, red eyes.

"Where's Doc Nielsen?" I said, lifting my chin to scan the crowd. "Surely he'd be here?"

"With fever on the rampage, I s'pect he's got his hands full."

One dead girl wasn't much of a rampage, but I forgot the doc when I noticed a second face was missing.

Elly's four uncles, Sam's older brothers, Bob, Ed, Earl, and Ray, all in their middle to late 70s, bent to clasp the wrought-iron casket hardware. With a heave, they brought the box to the cusp of the wood riser platform and slid it into place.

I could almost hear their backs creak. Earl let out a gasp, and each of them limped to the chairs reserved for them while the preacher took his place beside Elly's box.

While everybody got arranged, I scurried around to stand under the oak tree beside Riley.

"Have you seen Doc Nielsen?" I said. "Or Charlie Murry?"

"How much would you say Elly weighed?" said Riley, not making any effort to whisper.

Or answer my questions.

Doc was President of the Chamber of Commerce. He should be here.

And as close as they were, it was impossible that Charlie wouldn't be present.

But I suspected Big Sam was just as glad. The Murry's cattle operation was twice the size of the Benteen operation, and the two families were bitter rivals.

"Romeo and Juliet," I mused with a smile, but literary allusions were lost on my male comrades.

"Shush," whispered the clay-faced gravedigger at the fence. "We're gonna sing now."

"She wasn't a fat girl, was she?" said Riley. "Would you say Elly was fat?"

"Riley!"

"Certainly more than hundred pounds?" He scratched his head and watched a crow fly low over the seated crowd. "Maybe 130?"

"You best not let Big Sam hear you."

"I'd second that notion, friend," said the digger. "Take it from me, folks get mighty touchy about their dead. I mean, they could care less about somebody when they're alive and kicking, but after the drop off it's a whole 'nother story."

"We'll take that under advisement, thanks," I said.

"Would you say she was five feet tall? I think a bit more."

"More," I said. "Maybe five feet and four inches."

The assembled mourners started to sing "To Heaven I Lift Mine Eyes."

"Force times distance equals work," said Riley, gazing across the open prairie.

"Your boyfriend's quite a conversationalist," said the digger. "He always go on this way at funerals?"

Truth be told, I was just grateful Riley had taken the time to walk over and pay his respects.

I counted my blessings that he was dressed halfway decent.

That my dad had made Riley Boone a deputy lawman a few months before when he'd helped to solve a series of baffling crimes was frequently forgotten. He was young, only a year older than me, and he spent most of his time cooped up in his clock shop on the edge of town — a building occupied twenty years before by Thomas Edison when that erstwhile personage traveled to Wyoming to watch a solar eclipse.

Edison left all manner of notes and forgotten inventions that Riley tinkered with on a daily basis. To mangle an old saying, you could take the boy away from his science, but you couldn't take the scientist out of the boy.

"Mass times gravity equals weight," he said.

I nudged Riley in the ribs. "You didn't answer me about Doc Nielsen or Charlie Murry," I said.

"Under the willow," he said.

Following his gaze, I saw a lonely figure standing beside a horse under the open prairie's second tree.

"Why doesn't Doc join the crowd?" I wondered aloud. "You don't suppose he's quarantined himself?"

"That's just what I was thinking," said Digger with a serious nod. "Word is that it was him and only him that seen the girl after she passed. They didn't even let the undertaker have her for fear of contamination."

"Hence the closed casket," said Riley.

"Preacher's gonna talk," said Digger.

I'm not ashamed to say the Congregational minister wasn't familiar to me. He'd only recently moved to Randolph City with his family, and I haven't been much for churching since before my mom died.

With his puffed-up shock of silver hair and syrupy way of talking, I didn't think I was missing much not making his acquaintance.

"The Good Book says there is a time for all things. For comings and for goings. A time to be born and a time to die. The idea that our beloved Elly Benteen departed this early veil too soon is but the judgement of sinful pride. The truth is the Lord needed another angel, and who are we to question His grand design."

"Who indeed," said Digger with a sniff.

Riley held a pair of folding field glasses up to his spectacles. "I've got a question," he said.

I took the glasses when he offered them. "Look at the saddle on Doc Hamilton's mount."

180

Ignoring the drone of the preacher, I stared through the magnifying lenses at the richly thick leather, the polished pommel, the ornately decorated skirt and billet straps. The roan horse was a wonder as well. Strong and sleek with muscles that rippled in the sunlight, he was the equal of any prize stallion Sam Benteen might own.

But it had a Murry Ranch brand.

"Since Doc Nielsen moved to town, he's worked strictly on barter," I said. "He doesn't have two cents to rub together." Handing the glasses back to Riley, I declared, "That must be somebody else's horse and saddle."

"Or perhaps the doctor has come into some money," he said.

The preacher had finished his piece and it was time to lower Elly into the ground. Again, I watched her uncles teeter forward toward the coffin.

"Do you know that Bob and Earl helped me clean up some old iron behind the shop last week?" said Riley. "Neither of them can lift much of anything without giving out."

"So?"

"So if Elly weighs 130 pounds, plus something for the box —"

Before I knew it, Riley had taken three strides out of the oak tree's shade and rounded the mound of dirt.

I watched as he stepped in front of the four pall-bearers, stopping the service with an upturned hand. "If I might interrupt," he said. "For just a moment."

From his seat near the front, Dad spun around and gave me the stink-eye.

As if my impetuous friend's actions were my fault.

A gasp went up from the crowd as Riley bent down and knocked on the side of the box.

"Here, now. I won't stand for this," cried Big Sam.

"You won't have to," said Riley. "In fact," he said, straightening his back, "there's no need to continue with the service."

So transfixed was I with Riley's performance, I didn't notice the gravedigger move until he had a big, knuckled hand firmly clamped around my boyfriend's arm.

"You stop this nonsense right now," he said. "You're just making it harder for these good folk."

Riley looked at Digger's hand like it was a specimen under a microscope.

With graceful ease, he slipped out of his jacket, leaving his frustrated attacker holding an empty sleeve.

Digger raised his shovel, might've dropped

it on Riley's head too if not for my own interruption of the events.

The gun I carried under my petticoats was small and only held two shots. But at close range it would shatter the man's forehead.

"And I expect that's something you don't particularly want," I said after explaining it to him. I smiled mischievously at Riley. "But it might be something Mr. Boone is gonna get if he doesn't explain himself."

Riley returned my smile and nodded back toward the willow tree outside the cemetery.

I looked just in time to see Doc Nielsen on his horse, riding away from the scene as fast as his new saddle could carry him.

With a nimble flourish, Riley shoved Digger aside and, gripping the coffin handle nearest him, turned the box over with a terrific crash. The lid sprang open, and the sorrowful contents exploded across the new-mown grass.

Five-pound bags of flour.

"I suspect Charlie Murry and Elly Benteen are off making a life for themselves by now," said Riley as he drew a dripping tea strainer by its chain from his steaming cup.

We sat together at Dad's kitchen table, the still-gurgling kettle on a pad between us. Outside, the wind howled around the shutters and rattled the panes, but the clear, starlit night was hardly forbidding.

In fact, it suggested a romantic dalliance under the moon.

The Marshal of Randolph City was having none of that.

"What I want to know is how you could be so doggone sure of yourself," said Dad, pulling up a chair.

"It's simply a matter of physics," said Riley. "The amount of force it would take to carry a heavy body and casket the distance those old men managed. The effort shown by those gentlemen was almost Herculean when compared with what I've seen from them in the past."

"You don't think they noticed the load was lighter than it should've been?"

"You know the Benteen family hubris as well as anybody," said Riley. "I don't think their pride would let them admit it if they did."

"But still, you couldn't be sure. Can you imagine if you'd spilled the girl's body across the lawn in front of her grieving family? Not to mention exposing us all to the fever."

"There never was a fever, was there?" I said.

"I'm confident there wasn't," said Riley.

"Remember the gravedigger said only Doc Hamilton had seen the girl. I suspect his diagnosis was part of the entire ruse. After pronouncing her dead, he spirited her away to the Murry ranch. Or perhaps Charlie was waiting for her outside Doc's office."

Riley sipped his tea.

"While the Benteen family thought Doc was preparing Elly for burial, she was miles away, in the arms of her lover. Heir to a rival family."

"Sam Benteen will demand a posse," said Dad. "He'll want Doc Nielsen tracked down. He'll want somebody to pay."

"Curious at Sam's reaction today," said Riley. "He seemed more angry at being tricked than joyful that his daughter wasn't deceased."

I put my hand on his arm. "Remember what the gravedigger said? Folks could care less about somebody when they're alive and kicking, but after the drop off it's a whole 'nother story."

"It's more than that and you know it," said Dad. "There was another quotation today at the gathering. What the preacher said — about questioning the grand design of things."

I thought about Elly Benteen as we sipped our tea and listened to the night outside, the crickets chirping, spring peepers croaking, a coyote in the distance. All as much a part of the grand design as Elly Benteen and her lover.

And Sam would certainly be questioning that design tonight.

After all, Charlie — that is, *Charlene* — Murry was a girl.

THE MAHOGANY LILY

It was a dark and stormy night.

Inside his flooded cabin at River's Edge, up to his cadaverous ribs in a swirling brown tide, Ezra Baas struggled to keep a round mahogany picture frame pressed to his drenched, woolen shirt.

He pushed toward the open door.

The sorrowful wail of waterlogged timbers filled his ears as his home gave way to the onslaught of rain. Lightning lit the ravaged interior. Ezra dared glance over his shoulder.

Except for shirt, tattered pants, and the Sears, Roebuck frame clutched in his fingers — all was lost.

All he'd ever had, and all his sainted mother had brought from the old Dutch country, across the ocean, and across half a continent to the West.

Fine dining chairs of hand-hewn oak circled in Ezra's wake, struck with rigor, legs pointing skyward in death.

Loose pasteboard photos floated past on a skin of debris, lost in a stinking foam of churning river water.

The old mantel clock, washed from its perch.

A spinning wheel, listing like a ship to starboard.

Too much to save.

Ezra had waited too long, sure that the rain would stop.

Confident the mad river of 1908 would recede.

He stayed awake watching, but fell asleep.

He woke half-drowned.

And reached for the most important thing in the house.

The mail-order frame his mother called "The Mahogany Lily" with its protective glass and spun wire hanger.

Hung above her bed, it was the first thing the sun lit every morning, the last thing she saw each night.

Her eyes held the Lily even in death, her final words making Ezra promise to keep the piece always in the family.

He swore he would.

With renewed vigor, he thrashed against the tide, rocks and nails and who-knows-what slicing into the soles of his feet.

After an endless trek, he fell against a cottonwood south of the place, clinging to the tree with both arms, the treasured frame pushed tight between bark and wool shirt.

Exhausted, he felt pinned like Jesus on the cross.

But he'd saved The Mahogany Lily.

Salvation came with the morning sun and a patch of muddy red clay at the base of the tree.

The waters were receding, and Ezra retrieved the beloved picture frame from the ground beside him.

It was none the worse for wear.

"It's too bad about the little drawing inside," he said aloud.

Though it was nothing, really.

Just an old, old drawing mother used as a placeholder in books and finally stuck in the frame as something to show off.

"A drawing of Mary and Martha," she once told him. "Done by somebody one of our cousins knew in the old country. Somebody named Remberson or Rembrandt. Something like that."

Ezra peeled the tattered strips of paper from the glass and balled them up into a soggy wad.

He tossed the wad at a bird.

Mary and Martha didn't matter.
He had saved The Mahogany Lily.

A Bird's-Eye View

"Abracadabra," said Sheriff Cheyenne Ned, and the wind carried his words up and away across the open field of emerald springtime grass thirty feet below.

"What did you say?" said Mrs. O'Connor, with head back, eyes closed, a Tarot card pressed against her forehead. Long finger-nails, lacquered red and orange, reflected the early morning sun like fire.

"Just trying to help," he chuckled.

"Well, don't."

With braided black hair and dressed in a flowing white shirt and dark blue panta-loons, Mrs. O'Connor looked every bit the gypsy sorceress she purported to be.

Ned couldn't help but smile at the young lady's serious demeanor. The soft skin, the long lashes.

There was magic there alright, but it was biological more than supernatural.

Deputy Jim O'Connor was a lucky man.

To the left, and directly under them, the gleaming rails of the Standard Pacific railroad ran into the distance, and Sheriff Ned followed them with his eyes to the horizon. Up here perched on the boardwalk around Darbyville's railroad water tower, the breeze blew warm, promising a nice day.

It hadn't started that way.

It started in the cool dark of 5:30 a.m. with Deputy Jim banging on the Sheriff's door, waking him from a peaceful dream about their typically quiet western town.

"Looks like the railroad station's been hit again," Jim told him. "Somebody busted in after Old 55 went through. Frank says he locked up around midnight, but you ought to see the place now."

And he did.

When he arrived with Jim, the Sheriff saw broken windows, a smashed doorjamb and a wide-open steel safe, its contents mysteriously unmoved.

He saw it again in the first light of day.

He saw the station now, an hour later, as the sun climbed eagerly above the eastern row of cedars that bordered Hank Parson's farm place. Thirty feet long by twenty feet wide, the building boasted a new coat of white paint.

From this angle, Sheriff Ned saw it needed

a new rack of shingles.

He sighed.

Always something.

And this made it three weekends in a row that the place had been attacked.

"Who would want to smash up a train station?" he whispered to himself. "And why?"

"Shush," said Mrs. O'Connor, card still pressed to her head. "Shhh . . ."

At first, Sheriff Ned and his deputy had assumed they'd track the vandals quick enough.

But there were no leads to be found.

Repairs had been made, and then a week later, the depot was hit a second time. Just as before, nothing was removed, though plenty of railroad property saw considerable damage.

The two lawmen were stumped.

There were no clues. No motives.

That's when Jim suggested they consult with his wife.

Mrs. O'Connor was well known in the area for her uncanny abilities. From seeing the future to reading men's minds, folks called her a marvel, a witch, and worse.

Sheriff Ned called her his Consulting Detective.

He watched as a wagon carrying some men from Darbyville drove up the main street and stopped below.

"You getting anything, Clara?" he said.

Mrs. O'Connor nodded, nostrils flaring as she breathed in deep. Sheriff Ned kept his eyes above the girl's plunging neckline with its array of gold trinkets and carved beads.

"The culprit is there," she said, "below us."

As one, they leaned over the railing and took inventory on the crowd gathered below.

Four men had disembarked from the wagon to stand in a line next to Deputy Jim.

Closer to the building's boardwalk, Hank the stationmaster casually conversed with two women from the Lutheran Ladies' Aid.

Ben Lehigh, store owner, saw Ned and Mrs. O'Connor looking down. "How much longer you two going to be?" he called, hand cupped around the side of his mouth.

"We'll be down in a moment," said Ned.

"Careful on those steps," said Hank Parson.

"With Jim's wife? Are you kidding?" said Willy Hayes. "That bird can fly 'em down on her broom."

Jim took a menacing step toward the young towhead, but he had a smile on his face. "You watch it, Willy," he said before giving the kid's arm a thump.

"You know who did it?" said Dr. John Ellison.

Sheriff Ned queried Mrs. O'Connor with an arched an eyebrow.

"No doubt about it."

"Me too," he said, with a nod.

Then he answered the mayor of Darbyville. "Go ahead and grab hold of Hank Parson," he said. "Hold him until I get there."

The sheriff heard Hank's weak denials as he and Mrs. O'Connor moved toward the ladder.

"It makes sense," he said. "Hank owns property from his farm all the way down the rails to St. Martins, ten miles or more. I remember when the rail came to town, his papa tried to get the station on their property. Wanted to expand their produce market."

"He figured on forcing a relocation," said Mrs. O'Connor.

"He didn't figure on you," said Ned.

Mrs. O'Connor shrugged. "He should've waited until summer. When things are more dry."

Ned winked, and moved to climb down the water tower ladder ahead of her.

But not without first taking another look at the clue that had led to Hank Parson's undoing and that both of them had clearly seen from their high-altitude perch.

There, clearly visible in the rising sun, were two dark outlines in the morning dew where somebody had crossed the open grass between Hank's farm and the station and back again.

ACKNOWLEDGEMENTS

We write in rooms by ourselves, but nobody writes alone. Many thanks to Wayne D. Dundee, Brett Cogbum, Casey Cowan, Cheryl Pierson, Livia Washburn, John D. Nesbitt, James Reasoner, Peter Brandvold, Matt Mayo, and Paul Bishop.

And especially to Gina, Wyatt, Christyn, and Nora.

"Hester's Vanity" appeared in *Rough Country,* High Hill Press, 2013

"Storm Damage" appeared in *Sundown Western Tales,* Sundown Press, 2016

"The Scalper" appeared in *Western Tales,* Vol. 10, Cane Hollow Press, and won the Western Writers of America Spur Award for Short Fiction in 2016.

"Eustace and Cats" appeared in the Summer 2016 issue of *Saddlebag Dispatches,* Galway Press.

"Killing Hilda Kempker" appeared in the Autumn 2016 issue of *Saddlebag Dis-*

patches, Galway Press.

"AKA: The DaVinci Kid" appeared in the Autumn/Winter 2017 issue of *Saddlebag Dispatches*, Galway Press.

"Grand Design" appeared in the Spring/Summer 2018 issue of *Saddlebag Dispatches*, Galway Press.

ABOUT THE AUTHOR

After growing up on a Nebraska farm, **Richard Prosch** has worked as a professional writer and artist while in Wyoming, South Carolina, and Missouri.

His western crime fiction captures the fleeting history and lonely frontier stories of his youth, where characters aren't always what they seem and the wind-burnt landscape is filled with swift, deadly danger.

In 2016, Richard won the Spur Award for short fiction given by Western Writers of America.

Stop by and say hello at: www.Rich ardProsch.com, and be sure to join the newsletter posse or drop a line: richard@ richardprosch.com

CPSIA information can be obtained
at www.ICGtesting.com
Printed in the USA
BVHW040906161222
654388BV00010B/49